dancergirl

CAROL M. TANZMAN

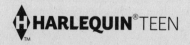

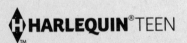

ISBN-13: 978-0-373-21040-4

DANCERGIRL

Recycling programs for this product may not exist in your area.

For Peter Cooper

His faith and quirky brilliance lit the way

prologue

You know the feeling you get when you're on the subway. Or a bus. Coffeehouse. Anyplace where people hang out. You're texting, or cramming the rest of your homework, when suddenly you feel…something. Back of the neck prickle, goose bumps all over your arms.

You glance up—and there he is. Some cretin, pupils burning, staring at you like he's got X-ray vision. Ripping through your clothes. Bra, panties—whatever turns the creep on. He catches your eye—that's what he's hoping to do—and then he does something gross. Draws his tongue over his lips, makes some crude smacking sound, gives a lewd wink. Immediately, you look down, pretending you haven't seen anything.

But you know he knows….

That's exactly what's happening. The sick feeling that someone's staring at me. Only I'm not on the subway. Or the bus. Or even a park bench.

I'm in my bedroom. Alone.

chapter one

"Question of the day," Jacy says. "What's the worst thing that could happen to you?"

Jeremy Carl Strode, aka Jacy, settles beside me on the worn marble stoop of the brick building we both call home. Jacy and his parents live on the fifth floor; Mom and I have the apartment above them.

"Alicia!" His bony elbow pokes me. Jacy's wearing the vintage AC/DC tee I gave him for his sixteenth birthday and a pair of ripped jeans. Knowing him, he's probably got on zero underwear because of the August heat wave.

"I heard you," I say. "Are you talking about school next year or, like, life?"

"Anything."

I fan my orange tank top over my stomach. "Is this for the *Gazette?*"

Just before classes ended in June, Jacy was named features editor at WiHi, our neighborhood public school officially known as Washington Irving High. He's in line for editor-in-chief when we're seniors *if* he can keep his father, "Mr. Go to MIT and Be An Engineer," out of his mop of curly hair.

"Let me think," I say.

"That'll take a while."

"Not everyone aces Calc in tenth, genius-man."

Jacy ducks his head in embarrassment and checks his cell. "Better get going if you want to show up to work on time."

In June, I'd scored a job at Moving Arts, the studio where I study dance. The sweetest part is that I can take as many classes as I want for free.

Halfway down the steps, Jacy trips and slides the rest of the way on his butt. My laugh cuts through the muggy air.

"Glad I amuse you," he mutters.

"All the time."

I give him a hand up and we head north past midsize apartment buildings, neat brownstones and the ethnic restaurants that, according to my mother, give the Heights its charm. Air-conditioned cars glide down the street, although the sidewalk is empty. The smell of garbage baking in metal cans is enough to cause the fainthearted to, well, faint.

"Got it!" I pull a rubber band from my messenger bag and twist my long, wavy hair into a ponytail. "Worst thing—it's the spring concert and the auditorium is sold-out. There's a scout from Merce Cunningham's company. I'm doing, like, fifteen pas de bourrée—" I demonstrate the step-side, cross-back, step-side move "—and then I trip. Not just a stumble but a humongous slip. The next thing you know, I'm sprawled facedown across the stage. God, how humiliating is that?"

The audience laughs. Samantha Warren gives a snarky smile as she completes her set of perfect pas de bourrée. I try desperately, awkwardly, to catch up to the count, knowing my entire career-to-be is ruined—

"I knew you'd say something like that." Jacy sounds triumphant. "You always think you're going to tank a performance."

"I could easily blow a dance!"

"Not ever!" Jacy insists.

Pleased, I coat my lips with French Vanilla ChapStick. We've reached the intersection of Clinton and Montague. Clothing boutiques, Trinity Church and upscale art galleries line the sidewalks. Moving Arts Dance Studio stands across the avenue, west of the subway entrance.

"What's *your* worst nightmare?" I ask.

No answer. Instead, Jacy steps off the curb—and that's when I see it. Without a doubt, he could do the math: *If an SUV travels at forty miles an hour and an idiot steps directly into its path, it would take X seconds to smash said idiot's brains—*

My arm shoots out. Desperate fingers pull his tee. "Watch out!"

A horn blares. Tires squeal. Jacy falls into the gutter with barely an inch to spare.

"Omigod!" I breathe. "Do you have any idea how close you came to roadkill?" He grins as he stands. "Don't laugh, Strode. It's, like, the third time you've done that since school let out!"

"Sorry."

"Sorry?" I jerk him around so he has no choice but to stare directly into my eyes.

"I didn't see the car," he mumbles. "It came down the street really fast."

"Not that fast. *I* saw it."

"So you're Superman with X-ray eyes and I'm not."

"Don't be a jerk," I say.

"I have to be someplace, and you're late." He makes a show

of looking both ways. "Is it safe to cross now, Mommy dear-est?"

I stare at him, and he actually waits for me to nod before stomping off toward the subway.

Now, how does that work?

Jacy's the one who does something stupid and I get snapped at. But that isn't the only thing that pisses me off. We've been together more than fifteen minutes, and he didn't bother to mention he's meeting someone.

Who? Jacy hasn't dated anyone since his spring breakup with Tiffany Kahlo. If he were hanging out with someone new, well, you'd think I'd be the first to know.

It's not like I'd be jealous or anything. Everyone knows it's a disaster to hook up with someone you've been friends with since third grade. A person you had to inform, at age twelve, that deodorant is a rather useful invention. Somebody you know goes commando on hot days and you don't even find it gross anymore. Put simply, Jacy and I have WTMI: Way Too Much Information about each other.

Whatever. By the time I enter Moving Arts, the line of tutu-skirted preschoolers waiting to check in for Fairy Tale Dance reaches halfway across the studio's air-conditioned lobby. The din is deafening, which is why I stamp at least fourteen class cards before realizing what should have been obvious.

What's the worst thing that can happen?

With the stunt he pulled out on the street, Jeremy Carl Strode clearly avoided having to come up with an answer.

That's when I decide there's a new question of the day.

What—or maybe *who*—is Jacy hiding?

chapter two

I'm in the middle of organizing class cards when I feel a presence at the other side of the reception desk. Lynette Williams, the studio's owner and a former professional dancer herself, points to the clock.

"If you're taking Quentin," she says, "go change. Lord knows you'd better be on time."

I hurry down the hallway. Another perk of working at the studio is that I have my own locker in the teachers' changing area. That means I don't have to get undressed in front of a million people. Baring my privates to a bunch of gossipy girls is not something that floats my boat.

Alone in the small room, I throw on my dance stuff and twist my hair into a bun. Its waviness comes from my mom. Although born in Puerto Rico, my mother and her family moved to Baltimore when she was a baby. After nursing school, Mom married a musician who was a mixture of Italian, African-American and, he claimed, a bit of Cherokee. They followed his dream to Brooklyn but he left town a year or so after I was born.

The mixed-salad heritage gave me almond eyes, full lips and a button nose—an "exotic look" my friend Clarissa says is "hot right now." Long legs help make battements, straight-legged kicks, my specialty. The Ballet I teacher used to call me "the Battement Queen." Jacy, however, thought I said "Batman's Queen." For years after, whenever we played superhero, my special power was the lightning-fast kick-to-the-villain's-head. Jacy picked laser fingers that could burn any object.

Right now, however, I wish I had the power of invisibility. Class has already started by the time I slip into Studio A.

"Nice of you to join us, Ms. Ruffino."

Quentin Carlyle, Modern IV's oh-so-fabulous teacher, is a Brit with a rep. It's mainly because he used to perform with Martha Graham's company, although it's obvious he had a lot of ballet. That's why he insists that everyone taking his class have enough classical training to keep up, which is fine with me. I started with ballet when I was little, before my mad love for Modern kicked in.

Quentin has short gray hair, a flexible body and a disapproving glare that tightens the muscles of even the best dancers. Definitely old-school, the Cranky Brit will bite the head off anyone who calls what he teaches "Contemporary." He always choreographs an unbelievable duet for the winter concert. The female part is the Moving Arts dream role.

"Back row." He points a slender finger. "Make it quick."

Samantha gives me her "poor baby" look—her concern so fake it's laughable. She'd gotten there fifteen minutes earlier to warm up on her own. Her parents are rich, so she doesn't have to stamp class cards and replace toilet paper before taking class.

Sam's practically anorexic, with silky hair that would make her a perfect choice for shampoo commercials—except for one thing. Her eyes. Not only are they two different colors—one is dark brown and the other ocean-blue—but the blue eye is almost double the size of the brown one. It's like God was playing Mr. Potato Head when she was created, got distracted by an earthquake or something so He pulled eyepieces from different sets.

Shooting her a "no problem in my life" smile, I settle between Keisha Watson, so shy she practically rents the last row, and "Check Out My Guns" Blake Russell. Blake's worried that someone will question his manhood. He works out—and flirts—constantly. He gives me his "you're so bad" wink, but I ignore him to concentrate on Quentin.

I live for this class. Even though the Cranky Brit's an obsessive-compulsive drill sergeant, hurling insults left and right, it's not only my technique that improves after every session. When I nail one of his combinations, the surge of confidence it gives me is unreal. It's as if Quentin has reached inside, pulled everything I'm good at and laid it right out there for all the world to see.

The floor warm-up ends. As we move to the round, wooden barre attached to the back wall for a series of parallel leg lifts, I glance at the mirrors lining the front of the room. Already, tendrils of hair have escaped my poorly twisted bun to curl into sweaty ringlets.

Quentin snaps his fingers. "Muscles adore heat, luvies. Streeetch."

After the barre, I down some water and watch him demonstrate the day's combination. Its quick leap comes out of an off-balance turn. It flows beautifully but is, I soon find out, extremely tricky.

Chaîné, coupé, jeté. Quentin choreographed the opening turn in bended-knee plié, not the half-toe lift a ballet teacher

would choose. It gives the combination a grounded beginning, so that the off-balance coupé, coupled with the big leap,
is more of a surprising contrast.

But it's hard. The room fills with the musky odor of hard
work and quiet concentration.

"Alicia!" Quentin's bark startles me. "You look like an
elephant. Shoulder toward your throwing leg, then bend
deeply as you land. And don't look at your feet! Demonstrate,
Samantha, that's a luv."

Her effortless leap ends with an elegant landing that barely
whispers against the wood. She gives me an oh-so-concerned
smile. "Do you want me to show you again?"

"I got it, thank you." My voice matches hers—poisoned
honey.

Quentin gives the rest of us the knotted-together, bushy-
eyebrow glare. "Same arm as leg, dancers. Right arm reaches
for the *right* leg!" Lightbulb-popping "ohs" circle the room as
several people make the adjustment.

He raps his knuckles on the mirror. "Fours across the floor.
There's room for three sets, back to front on the diagonal. And
don't forget. Make it your own or you'll never get out of the
corps!"

Make it my own? I'm still having trouble making it cor-
rectly. I slink into the last group alongside Keisha. With her
long neck and perfect cheekbones, she looks like Ethiopian
royalty. She's also way too talented to hide in the back. Then
again, Keisha's several years younger than the rest of us, so
that might explain why she's such a shrinking violet.

She and I mark the combination while the quartets travel
across the floor. "Down, down, turn," I mumble as each
group starts. When it's our turn, I start off fine but somehow
screw up so I end behind the beat.

What's wrong with me? I'm the only one in the room who can't figure it out. Not only that, but Samantha's next cross is flawless. She twists her wrist to give the leap an extra flair. Everyone watches, and not because of her giant blue eye. Already, it's obvious that the winter duet is Sam's to lose.

As I mimic the quartet ahead of me, Keisha shakes her head. "You're adding an extra chaîné after the first jump, Ali. Two steps, not three."

Aha! That explains why I start off fine but get behind halfway across the floor. I give Keisha a grateful nod as we get into place.

5-6-7-8

The beat drives my muscles. Halfway across the room, I hit the timing of the second leap just right and find myself airborne. Yes! With toes pointed hard, I finish strong, controlling the landing.

The next two crosses are heaven. I don't think about anything. Not Samantha, not the duet, not my feet. I'm catapulted straight into the never-never land of pure dance, where music and movement are the only things in the world that exist. I could stay here forever....

I land the final plié soft as whipped cream. Quentin's eyebrows rise, his version of a nod of approval.

Class ends. Dancers applaud, Quentin bows. Samantha gives me a stony glare and storms off to the dressing room. She hates it whenever the Cranky Brit notices anyone but her.

Blake palms me a sweaty low five. Samantha dumped him just before the spring concert so he gets off whenever she's pissed—which is most of the time.

He wraps a towel around his neck. "Want to get a slice at Tony's?"

I try not to laugh. All Anorexic Sam eats is fat-free frozen yogurt. Not exactly he-man food.

"Can't. My mom's made dinner."

I drain the last of the water bottle and float into the teachers' dressing room. As soon as I get home, I plan to work on the combination in my bedroom. Slow it down some, then speed it up. Just for fun, I want to see how fast I can actually—

Bang!

The sound echoes like a gunshot in the small room. Half-naked, I bring my leotard to my chest.

"Sorry." Eva Faus, the petite, thirtysomething choreography instructor, stands next to a full-length, now-closed locker door. "Thought you saw me."

"Wasn't paying attention."

She eyes my sweaty leotard. "Quentin?"

"He's killer."

"That's 'cause the man's got chops. I saw him dance years ago. God, he's beautiful onstage." Eva wears a green unitard. With her spiky hair and nose ring, she reminds me of a punked-out forest nymph. "You haven't taken any choreography classes, have you?"

It's not really a question.

"I'm not sure I'm ready."

She laughs. "Oh, you're ready. I saw you in Mara's trio last spring—lovely. There's room in the fall class. You should sign up."

Holy moly! Nobody just "signs up" for Choreography. You have to get Eva's permission, which, apparently, I just did.

A mental bow to Quentin. There's no way I'd have gotten this good without Modern IV—*his* Modern IV class. After Eva leaves, I do my happy dance, something like a salsa. Feet moving to the beat in my head, I sprinkle baby powder over my body before slipping back into the orange tank and denim skirt. Then I check my cell. Two text messages. Clarissa: What's up? And another from my friend Sonya: Godfather marathon. Nothing from Jacy.

My flip-flops make soft, slapping sounds as I head home. A slight breeze has sprung up and the street pulses with movement.

In my blissed-out, after-class state, dance is everywhere. Pedestrians swarm out of the subway, an urban line dance snaking past the fruit stand. Pigeons diving for bread crumbs create a swooping pattern more intricate than the New York City corps de ballet. Kids play hopscotch chalked onto the sidewalk, the rhythmic jumping its own music: two, one, one. Two, one, one. Two.

The bodybuilder doing curls in front of a second-story window, muscular arms pumping, keeps a steady tempo: up, down. Beat. Up, down. Beat. He catches my eye and winks. I hurry across Clinton.

Mr. Ryan, recently retired, sits on a folding chair in front of his brownstone. He wears collared, buttoned-down shirts all year, long-sleeved in the winter, short-sleeved in the summer, but it's his fingers, tap-dancing on a laptop, that grab my attention.

He glances up. "Hot enough for you?"

"Really. Do you know when it's supposed to break?"

"Not till after the weekend," he says.

Maybe I can get Jacy, Clarissa or Sonya to do a Sunday matinee at the Quad. Doesn't matter what we see; AC all afternoon sounds good to me.

Up ahead, Jacy lounges on the stoop, grocery bag at his side. His hair, frizzed by the humidity, looks like a clown's wig.

"Your hair is a beast, Strode."

He shrugs. "I've been waiting forever."

"Didn't know I was late."

Clearly, Jacy's not mad anymore. Still, I'd like to know where he went. "Whatcha do today?"

"Nothing much," he says. "But I've got a surprise for tonight."

"Yeah? What's in the bag?"

"Picnic stuff. Reggae at the band shell. Sonya and Clarissa are already there."

I glance up. The brick structure was built in the early 1900s when six floors was a big deal. Now, it's just another old building housing a mixture of rent-control holdouts like me and Mom, and newer people who pay zillions to live in the same-size apartments.

"I already talked to your mom," Jacy says. "She's cool as long as we get back by ten and you beep her the minute you get in."

Mom, a charge nurse for Mercy Hospital, works the night shift. She usually leaves the apartment by nine o'clock. Cell phones aren't allowed in hospitals so we have a beeper code that I cannot forget to use—or I'm in big trouble. 04, for OK, means "I'm home." 78 is short for "running late." And 505—SOS—means "I need help." I've never needed that one, although as Mom says, "This *is* Brooklyn. The crazies are everywhere."

I shake my head. "Have to shower before I go anywhere."

Jacy buries his nose in my neck.

"Stay away from the pits!" I shriek.

"You don't smell bad. Forget the shower. Seize the moment."

"You always say that when you want to do something at the last possible second," I grumble. "You know I like to—"

"Plan. But this is the last concert of the summer. The *Voice* gave it two stars."

"I thought you were boycotting the *Voice*."

"Things change."

Yeah, they do. Then again, some things don't. If Jacy doesn't want you to know about something, there's no way you'll know. Unless, of course, you do a little bit of detective work on your own.

chapter three

We enter Prospect Park at Ninth Street. A group of Dominican men are heavy into a soccer game, children swarm all over the playground and barbecued meat perfumes the air.

My stomach growls so loud Jacy laughs. "And you call me a beast!"

The crowd follows the asphalt path around the ranger station. The white band shell sits at the bottom of a natural amphitheatre. A Celebrate Brooklyn! banner spans the lighting rig. People are everywhere; blankets laid out end to end create a giant chessboard. The spicy scent of weed drifts on the breeze.

"Jacy!" Sonya shouts. "Over here!"

I spot her first. She and Clarissa have staked out a prime spot under a tree. Jacy and I thread our way up the hill.

Sonya's soft, pillowy skin reminds me of the Pillsbury Doughboy. She counters that with some major body piercing: nose, tongue, belly and, at last count, seven earrings on each lobe. Her eyes, lined with dark makeup, are huge.

But not as huge as her appetite. "What did you bring?"

Jacy sets the grocery bag on the blanket and removes a dozen doughnuts, six-pack of Coke and the grapes I insisted we buy at the corner market.

"Awesome," Sonya says. "Clarissa and I got hummus, pita and cucumber salad from that Middle Eastern place on Fourth. And a box of Mrs. B's cookies."

A true-blue fashionista, Clarissa is doing a Guatemalan-peasant thing: white embroidered blouse tied to bare her midriff, low-slung jeans. She has a deal with a stylist in the Village and gets free haircuts if she lets the guy experiment. This time, her hair is a mixture of lengths—real short on the right side, longer on the left. Not one of the better cuts, but not as bad as the one where her scalp looked like it got caught in a blender.

Someone jumps Jacy from behind. "Strode!"

Josh Tomlin, who was Banquo in the school's hip-hop version of *Macbeth,* does the WiHi handshake: palm slide, fist smack. Not quite the pretty boy he thinks he is—his jaw is way too square—he might actually have some acting talent underneath all that ego. Charlie Liu, on the other hand, is skinny and hyperactive, with square-framed glasses that are a little too big for his face. Video camera in one hand, he rattles a bucket of Kentucky Fried with the other.

"Jace the Ace," Charlie says. "Join the fiesta?"

Clarissa, Sonya and I make room on the blanket.

"You didn't tell me it was a party!" I whisper to Jacy.

He gives me a wicked grin. "Didn't know who would show."

Now I *really* wish I'd showered—but as soon as the band begins to play, I forget all about it. Sinewy bass, syncopated drums. By the time I finish eating, Clarissa moves to the groove.

"Dance with me," she cries.

She doesn't have to ask twice. I start small to allow reggae's seductive rhythm to settle into my bones, and then let my body go where it wants. Doesn't take long before the world melts away. Just me, the music and—

It.

Back of the neck prickle, goose bumps on my arms. I swivel around. Everywhere, people are mellow. Lying on blankets. Getting high. Batting a beach ball through the crowd.

My friends are occupied, too. Sonya, still sitting by the food, laughs at something Josh says. Jacy leans against the base of the tree, talking to Laura Hernandez. She came to the concert with Luke Sorezzi's stoner crowd.

At last, I notice Charlie farther up the hill, channeling Spike Lee, Minicam trained on me.

It's exactly like my dream, only this time someone really *is* staring. It totally weirds me. Performing onstage is one thing; being secretly *observed,* like I'm some kind of zoo animal, is something else.

Busted!

Charlie sees me staring, hands on hips. Immediately, he turns the camera toward the stage. My groove broken, I walk over to Jacy and Laura Hernandez.

"Yo!"

"Grab the cookies," Jacy tells me.

I toss the box into his hands. Laura gives me a "Get lost!" stare. She's got raven hair and flashing eyes, but I don't like the way she's practically sitting in his lap. Way too pushy.

When I don't move, she stretches in a way designed to show off her considerable rack. She's wearing a spaghetti-strap tank that she's practically busting out of. "Guess I'll bring that record over tomorrow."

Jacy nods. "Sounds good."

She gives me a triumphant glare and waltzes back to Sorezzi.

I nibble a pecan sandie. "Score a hot date?"

Jacy shrugs. "Whatever. Are you having fun?"

"Yeah. This was a good idea."

"Told you." He gropes the cookie box and surfaces with the last one. "Want to hear my news?"

"You have news?"

"You are now looking at the *Voice*'s fall intern," he announces.

"No way."

Jacy was a finalist for the summer one but lost out at the last moment, which explains his slacker vacation.

He grins so wide, his dimples look as if they're chiseled into his cheeks. "Let's dance."

Now *that's* almost as amazing as the internship. I've never seen Jacy volunteer to dance with anyone. The band segues into a Marley song and the crowd begins to sway as one, so sweet it's like floating in a bowl of caramel syrup. Jacy catches the mood. He leans forward, an odd gleam in his eye.

Omigod! Is he going to kiss me?

Just as the question forms, a beach ball comes at us from the left. Instinctively, I move back. The ball smashes Jacy's nose.

"Ooof," he breathes, more surprised than hurt.

"Why didn't you duck?"

With a laugh, I bat the ball down the slope. By the time I turn around, Jacy's back against the tree, looking extraordinarily pissed off. At the ball? Himself? Me?

I shouldn't have laughed. Immediately, however, my mind skips from shouldn't to couldn't. As in: he *couldn't* have been about to kiss me. I know he's happy about the internship but nobody, and I mean nobody, kisses their best friend, for the very first time, in public.

chapter four

I wake up the next morning convinced I'm crazy. There's no way Jacy was about to kiss me. He probably leaned forward to make some comment about his own dancing.

That's when a truly horrible idea strikes. Maybe Jacy thought *I* was about to kiss *him* and that's why he sat back under the tree.

My worry deepens when he doesn't show up at the stoop. I wait as long as I can but end up walking to work alone. He doesn't text all day, doesn't return mine. When I leave the studio, there aren't any voice messages. The front steps are empty.

I crowd into the elevator with the Russian computer geek, old Mr. Detwiler, his brown Chihuahua and a packed grocery cart.

The Russian is reading the newspaper. He's mastered the NYC subway accordion; three long folds. A headline pops out: Massive Manhunt for Montana Teen. Guess Brooklyn's not the only place you need a 505 trouble code.

I almost jump out of my skin when Mr. Detwiler pats my shoulder. His hand lingers a bit too long for my liking.

"Did you have a nice day, dear?" he asks.

His wife died recently, so everyone in the building feels bad for him.

"Yes, thank you," I lie. "Did you?"

I don't listen to the answer. My index finger hesitates at the five button but then moves to six. Nothing happened last night so it's not like I can knock on Jacy's door and apologize. I can't bring up the subject of kissing. Ever.

Both the Russian and Mr. Detwiler exit at three. I come back to earth long enough to say goodbye. At six, I hurry down the hallway. Sometimes, Jacy comes up to the apartment to wait for me. He doesn't mind talking to Mom.

After unlocking the door, I yell, "I'm back."

The "no one's home vibe" is obvious. Mom's note, sitting on the kitchen table, confirms that I'm alone: "Covering a shift. Dinner in fridge."

I eat in front of the TV, and then move to my room. It's the smaller of the two bedrooms but it's at the front of the building so I've got a view of Clinton instead of the back alley. My bed hugs the wall opposite the window. Next to the bed are my desk, clock radio and computer. Above the computer is a shelf with a collection of dolls wearing traditional costumes from around the world.

Jacy hasn't added anything to his blog since the day before yesterday. He posts every night but for some reason, he hasn't gotten around to writing about his internship—or the concert.

Charlie, however, sent a Zube link. The outlaw share site is the coolest thing on the net—no corporate commercials masquerading as someone's "home" videos.

The film starts with a low shot of the band. Next, Charlie alternates wide angles and close-ups. The camera pans the crowd. Ooh—there I am, dancing. Charlie zoomed in so close you can't see Clarissa and cut away before I flipped him off.

I click Replay and watch myself critically. Really good rhythm and a nice Martha Graham contraction I don't remember doing. I reach for my cell but it rings before I can grab it.

"Hey, Charlie. I was just watching the video."

"You like?"

"Yeah, actually. It came out pretty good."

"Excellent. Want to do another? Just you."

"You mean, only me dancing?" I pause to consider. "Jacy said that was the last concert."

"It doesn't have to be at the band shell. I can shoot someplace else. A party. One of your classes."

"You sure?"

"Are you kidding? This video's going viral. Five hundred views in the last hour. You could be famous."

"I guess. If you really think it's a good idea…"

"Awesome!" he says. "Let me get back to you when I figure out what I want."

I'm so pumped, I skip the elevator and charge down the stairwell to Jacy's apartment. No one answers the doorbell so I knock loudly.

"Anyone home? It's Ali." The inner chain unhooks. "Mrs. Strode!"

Jacy's mom looks terrible. Her honey-blond hair, usually tastefully combed, is a mess. Streaks of black under her eyes mean her mascara has run but she hasn't bothered to fix it.

"Is everything okay?" Dread smashes into my stomach like a dodgeball I haven't dodged. "Is Mr. Strode—"

"I'm fine."

Now Mr. Strode comes to the door. A senior accountant for a large downtown firm, he never leaves his office before 8:00 p.m.

"We just got in ourselves." His voice sounds hollow, as if the charcoal business suit he wears has turned to tin. Even his skin looks gray.

Uh-oh. Parental fight.

I want to get out of the way, quick. "Jacy home?"

The Strodes exchange a look.

"He's in his room," Mrs. Strode says. "But—"

"Thanks."

I scoot through the living room. Jacy's bedroom is directly below mine. "Jace? It's Ali."

At the sound of a grunt, I open, and then close, the door. I half expect him to be watching the video, assuming Charlie sent him the link, too, or working his blog. Instead, Jacy sits on the windowsill, staring at the fire escape.

"Turn on your—" I stop when he swings around. His eyes are rimmed with red. "Hey! Don't take it so hard."

He blinks. "What?"

"Your folks. I know they're fighting, but they're not like Mom and Andrew. When Mom and Andrew were together, that is." I sit at Jacy's desk. "I want to show you something—"

"My parents aren't—"

His laptop is so fast the footage comes up in seconds. "Look! I'm on Zube."

Jacy kicks his bed. "You are unbelievable. Always thinking about Alicia Ruffino."

The tone is clear. He is seriously pissed off.

"Right," I tell him. "I'm the selfish one."

"What's that supposed to mean?"

"Who drops everything because you feel like going to a concert? Who saved you from being squashed by a car? You didn't even bother to tell me where you were going, did you? And who came up with an answer to that stupid question yesterday—"

"Is that what you think I am?" he shouts. "Stupid?"

The bedroom door swings open.

"Jeremy?" Mr. Strode says. "Everything all right?"

My face grows hot with embarrassment. Jacy's obviously in one of his moods, and I know better than to try and reason with him.

"It's okay, Mr. Strode. I was just leaving."

chapter five

Back in my apartment, my cell buzzes. The texts don't stop until after midnight. The video was linked all over the place. Everyone thinks I look great.

In the morning, though, it's Jacy that's on my mind. Something was wrong last night, and not letting him talk first was rude. I text him: I'm an idiot. Call me.

He doesn't. I check online. Not a single blog entry since the day before the concert.

Again, I skip the elevator and take the steps. No one answers when I ring the bell or after I knock. I press my ear to the door but all is quiet.

It occurs to me that Jacy might have been telling the truth about his folks. Which means that if the Strodes weren't fighting, something was bothering them, too. Perhaps Mr. Strode found out about the *Voice* internship and he won't let Jacy do it if he has to drop Discrete Mathematics, which maybe ten other kids in the history of high school have taken.

Or Mr. Strode's company got downsized and he lost his job. Or Jacy's grandmother died. Whatever it is, Jacy refuses to return a phone call, text message or email the rest of the week.

I do some detecting. That means hanging around the building lobby to ask the postman if the Strodes filled out a "hold the mail" vacation card—they didn't—and then calling Josh and Charlie to see if they heard from him. Neither of them knows what's going on. It's like Jacy, and his family, dropped off the face of the earth.

chapter six

Charlie calls ten minutes after the invite goes out on the net. Sonya's having an end-of-summer party and he wants to make sure I'll be there.

"It'll be on the roof," he tells me. "The footage will be awesome!"

City roofs are amazing. You can watch a sunset, secretly smoke or just plain hide out. When parents are on the war-path, they never think to check the roof.

Sonya's is better than most. The perfect party place. Unlike my building, with its two-foot lip, her roof has a five-foot wall surrounding the edge. No matter how wasted someone gets, they'd have to try really hard to fall off.

The day of the party, Clarissa decides to play stylist. She brings over a bunch of clothes from her closet. We go with a pretty V-neck and short skirt. Makeup and hair take another hour but in the end, I'm happy with the look.

By the time we get to Sonya's, the party is in full swing. Word obviously got out on some site or other because I don't even recognize half the people. They're packed together like at the Thanksgiving parade when the Snoopy balloon floats by. Cell phones and cameras snap as people dance and clown—a last hurrah. Clarissa and I elbow our way through the crowd, searching for Charlie. When we finally meet up, he gives me the once-over.

"Blue's an excellent choice for the camera," he pronounces.

"Hi to you, too," Clarissa says. "And thanks. I picked out the shirt."

I look from one to the other. I might as well be uncooked tofu for all they care. A little annoyed, I spot the cooler, grab a beer. Charlie follows. He points to an empty spot near the ledge.

"I like the lighting over there. Very end-of-the-world sci-fi."

Suddenly, I'm extremely thirsty. I slug some beer. "What do you want me to do exactly?"

"Just dance, be natural. And make sure not to look at me."

Before I can move, Luke Sorezzi strolls over. He's dressed all in black and his hair has that "I don't give a crap so I finger-comb" look.

"Yo, Ruffino. Saw the video on Zube. You looked good."

He hands me a joint and I toke deeply. Even if I wasn't worried about the video, there's something about Luke that brings out the nerves in me.

"Yeah, well, I didn't know anyone was taping me," I mumble.

"Riiiighht." Luke smirks.

"I'm serious."

"Then it's just natural talent. The best kind."

Over in the corner, Charlie's giving me the "hurry up" sign. I hand Luke the joint. "Thanks for the hit. Umm, nice talking to you."

"Hold on. The school's best dancer deserves a little extra."

Luke tokes deeply and pulls my head toward his. As my mouth opens in surprise, he blows smoke into me. I blink, not sure whether it's the weed or the fact that his lips are so casually pressed into mine. Then he strolls away like he's done that every day for a month instead of the truth—before the Zube video, he never even noticed we breathe the same sooty Brooklyn air.

"Alicia!" Charlie has come to get me. "I've been waiting."

A final gulp of beer before we move to the chosen spot.

"Hold on, Charlie. You want me to dance by myself? Who does that?"

"You do. Well, not you, but the girl in my video. She's a free spirit—think Audrey Tautou in *Amelie*."

"Never saw it."

Charlie waves it off. "Doesn't matter. Don't think you. It's just…a dancer girl. And remember, don't look at me."

He backs off so you can't even tell what—or who—he's shooting. Not that anyone would notice. There's a surge over by the cooler. Someone, I take it, has managed to scam more beer and the crowd is ecstatic.

Clarissa gives me an encouraging smile. I take a breath, about to start, when a window curtain shifts in the tall building across the alley. At least I think it does.

"Ready when you are," Charlie announces.

Chills crawl down my spine. "I feel like I'm in a Macy's window display right here. Can't we move?"

"Fine!"

Charlie picks a different spot, still on the far end of the roof, but not so close to the alley. Just as I start, he yells, "Wait up."

He motions Josh over, placing him and Clarissa so there's a

barrier between me and the party. That's so no one can stumble into the shot.

I begin again. Being videotaped is like being onstage. Nerve-racking at first but then the movement, and adrenaline, of performance take over and something magical happens.

Two songs later, Josh approaches. "Can I join you? Or does that mess with your concentration?"

Out of the corner of my eye, I see Charlie give me the thumbs-up. "Guess not."

Josh's face lights up. Did he do this on his own—or did Charlie send him? Either way, I worry that my freestyle is boring, so I kick it up a notch by double-timing everything. Josh sweats buckets trying to keep up.

After another song, I'm done. I head for the Styrofoam cooler and check out the party. Sorezzi's in the southeast corner, surrounded by a circle of "admirers." Clearly, he came to the party to do a little business of his own.

Clarissa bustles over. "Charlie let me see the playback. The outfit's perfect. I'm sure he'd let you see—"

"Yo!" Sonya weaves over to us, well on her way to getting trashed. "Having fun?"

"Sonya!" Clarissa squeals. "Did you see Charlie shooting Ali?"

"Uh-uh. I was talking to Laura Hernandez. Why? What happened?"

She spots Charlie but it's Josh, intently watching the playback, who makes Sonya's face turn brittle. It suddenly penetrates that she spent most of the reggae concert talking to Josh.

Uh-oh. Sonya has a habit of crushing on the wrong guy and getting scorched in the process.

"Nothing happened," I inform her. "And to answer your question, it's an awesome party."

"I guess." Sonya's buzz is gone. She ducks down, roots through the cooler. "Laura asked about Jacy. Is he coming?"

"Haven't talked to him since Wednesday. We sort of had a fight."

Clarissa's eyes widen in expectation of a gossipy score. "What about?"

"Who knows? You know how Jacy gets. I stopped by the apartment earlier today, but nobody was home. Again."

Sonya pulls a forty from the cooler. "Maybe he went to the Shore. Don't his parents have a place in Wildwood?"

"Yes, but you'd think he'd have mentioned he was going. Or texted back. I've left, like, three messages."

"It's Jacy we're talking about. He probably left his phone charger under a heap of dirty laundry." Clarissa shudders. "I don't know how he gets away with that."

"If they're at the Shore, why didn't his folks hold the mail?" I demand.

"Because they forgot?" Sonya pops the top from the forty before she and Clarissa head off to find chips.

I think about Jacy's red eyes, Mrs. Strode's mascara-streaked cheeks. The kiss that wasn't a kiss. Something's going on, and I want to know what it is.

It takes two days for Charlie to edit the party footage. After he posts, I watch it in the privacy of my bedroom.

Charlie invented a character. *Shyboy101*. He saw me at the band shell but was too afraid to approach. Then he shows up at the party. The camera pans across the back of Sorezzi lighting up and there I am. As I dance, drink beer and talk to my friends, we hear *shyboy*'s voice-over.

"There she is—*dancergirl*. But she doesn't even notice me. To her, I'm invisible. Should I go up to her, say something? Not a chance! All I can do is watch from afar. Hoping that one day, she'll see me.

"Until next time, this is *shyboy101*."

It's surprising how real it looks. Like there's truly a *shyboy* who never met *dancergirl,* let alone talked to her. The fact that I didn't look at the camera really does make *shyboy* seem invisible. And since everyone, well, everyone except maybe Luke Sorezzi, has felt like a nobody at one time or another, the audience can't help but root for *shyboy* to talk to the cool girl.

Cool girl being…me?

Which is a joke. I've never been anyone's idea of cool, unless you count the Fairy Tale Dance kids. The little ones think I rock, but that's not saying much. Still, it's fun to see myself on the screen—although I spend the next four views critiquing my dancing. Not bad, but I could do better.

The only drawback is that I can't show Mom. She'll kill me if she discovers both the weed and the beer. She has a *serious* thing about underage…well, underage anything.

Then there's Strode. Wherever he is, if he doesn't have his cell, I certainly hope Jacy's got his laptop—and a decent connection to the net.

chapter seven

My heart races. Breathing is quick, shallow. Adrenaline courses through my body—but not the good kind of performance adrenaline. It's the get-out-of-here-quick kind. Fight or flight, the bio book called it.

But there's no one to flee from and nobody to fight. Unless you count the ratty stuffed animals I share the bed with.

Why am I having nightmares? Even spookier is that I can't always remember what's in them. All I know is that suddenly I'm wide-awake, practically screaming because someone stares at me. Like I'm a jellyfish in the Coney Island Aquarium. Or one of *Los Desaparecidos,* The Disappearing Ones, in the Spanish III documentary on Argentina.

There was this part about torture that's hard to forget. The police used electric prods and then buckets of water to fake-drown the prisoners. Sometimes they kept the lights on 24/7. Watched the captives constantly, waking them up whenever they fell asleep.

When we saw the film, the lights-on thing hadn't seemed

so bad. At least not compared to other kinds of torture. Now I'm not so sure....

Being stared at 24/7? Oh, yeah, that would drive me nuts. I'd tell anyone anything just to get them to leave me alone.

chapter eight

Turns out, Brooklyn has its own *Los Desaparecidos*. Or at least three: Jeremy Carl Strode and his folks.

On the morning after Labor Day, I walk to WiHi alone. Jacy's never missed a first day of school in his life. That, along with the lack of sleep, makes me crazy.

I get a bit distracted when I see the mob scene. The high school's wide marble stairs are filled with nervous freshmen, high-fiving sophomores and juniors, cheek-kissing seniors. Everyone stalls, knowing that the instant you step through the doorway, summer is truly dead.

A whispered conversation catches my attention.

"That's *dancergirl!*"

"Told you she goes here."

Two ninth-graders eyeball me. Obviously, Charlie's videos made the rounds of the new kids but someone should have told them that staring is so middle school.

It's like that all morning. Seniors nod in the hall like they know me, people in class who I've never talked to before start up conversations. It's wild to suddenly be Miss Popularity and takes the sting away from the fact that I get nightmare Mr. Han for Algebra II. Even Jacy had a hard time understanding the guy when he got stuck with him for Pre-Calc.

I go room to room in the hope that Jacy will be in English or American History with me. I'm disappointed each time. His name is not on any class list.

At noon, Sonya and I meet at our usual place near the hot-lunch line. I pretend not to notice the nudges and stares-which-aren't-stares that follow us as we carry our trays through the cafeteria to Josh's table.

Sonya maneuvers next to him. Before I can ask if either of them have any classes with Jacy, Clarissa hops onto the bench. She must have spent hours putting together her first-day-of-eleventh-grade outfit: vintage designer jacket, scooped-neck tee, rocker jeans.

"I've been looking for you all day, Ali. The whole school has seen your dancing. It's all anyone wants to talk about."

"I checked during study hall," Josh offers. "Over fifty thousand hits. You're, like, famous and stuff."

"*Totally* famous," Sonya says.

Is that sarcasm, along with ketchup, that she's squirting over her hamburger?

"And speaking of people," she adds, "has anyone seen Jacy today? Is the dude even alive?"

"My question exactly." I lean in. "It's like he disappearado'ed."

Clarissa's polished fingernail slits open a juice container. "Luke Sorezzi told Laura Hernandez who told me in Bio that Jacy was arrested."

"What for?" I ask. "Knowing all the answers to the math test?"

Josh waves a soggy French fry. "Maybe he's pregnant. Back in the day, girls disappeared from school all the time."

Clarissa smacks Josh's head just as Charlie stops beside our table. He sets his camera on the edge. "If it's Strode you're discussing, I talked to him."

"When?" Clarissa demands.

"Ran into him at the park yesterday," Charlie says.

"He's home?" My voice comes out squeaky, so I gulp some juice.

"Yeah. His dad's making him go to some private school in Manhattan."

I choke. Everyone stares until my coughing fit stops—but whether it's because orange juice spurts from my nose or because I'm clueless about Jacy is anyone's guess.

Clarissa leans in. "He didn't tell *you?*"

Josh saves me from an embarrassing answer. He taps Charlie's camera. "Were you taping us?"

Charlie shrugs.

"Omigod!" My hand automatically pats my hair. "You should tell me first."

"Didn't think you'd mind. We've blown up!"

"It still might be nice to know when you're shooting."

Josh grins. "It's better this way. More natural, right, Charles? Did you get me in the shot? Can I pretend to be Ali's boyfriend?"

The bell rings and the cafeteria explodes with movement.

Charlie grabs my arm. "We've got to talk. I have a bunch of ideas—"

"Dancergirl!" The taller of the morning's ninth-graders runs toward me.

Charlie swears. "Can't be seen with you. I'll call."

He takes off.

"Was that *shyboy?*" the girl asks, breathless. "Did he finally talk to you?"

"Uh, no."

"He had a camera."

"Yeah. Lots of kids have cameras," Clarissa offers. "There's a film class. You can take it in eleventh."

The girl seems disappointed but then brightens. "Can I get your autograph?"

"Seriously?" I don't know whether to feel embarrassed for me, or her.

Clarissa nudges my arm.

"Um, okay. Sure, I'll sign something," I mumble.

The girl snatches paper from her folder, fumbles for a pen.

I start to write *Ali,* then stop. "Do you want my real name?"

She looks at me as if I'm the idiot. "Of course not. Just say, 'To Tanya. Isn't it cool we go to the same school? Love, *dancer-girl.*'"

I write what she wants except instead of *love,* I scribble *from.*

"Thanks." She takes off, waving the paper. "Julie! Look."

Her morning friend stands by the garbage cans.

I turn to Clarissa and Sonya. "Let's get out of here before I have to sign Julie's paper-bag book cover."

"But I want your autograph, too." Sonya makes a show of searching through her backpack. "I'm sure I have an unused tampon."

Clarissa laughs. "You'd probably make a lot of money selling it on eBay."

I shudder. "Don't even go there!"

chapter nine

After the last bell, I head down Montague Street. Tony's Pizzeria, two doors from the studio, has a line of kids waiting to get the "slice and soda" after-school special. To avoid the crowd, I swing into the gutter and almost trip over a biker dude.

"Sorry!"

"No problem."

The guy leans against a chrome-and-leather Harley parked in the no-parking zone. He's cut, forearms bulging with knotted muscle. Despite the cool September weather, he has rolled-up sleeves with a bunch of tats poking out, and his cheeks sport a day-old-shave thing. Startling blue eyes check me out.

He winks. "Break up with your boyfriend?"

"Excuse me?"

"Curly-haired bloke. Yay high. Haven't seen him around lately."

"Jacy? He's not—" A warning flashes. "How do you—"

"Know who you are? Babe like you? Besides the fact that

I'm the one who pointed you out to Eva last spring, you're all over Zube." His blue eyes move down my body. "Pretty impressive, *dancerchick*." He smiles. "What can I say? I'm like *shyboy*. Got a nose for dancers."

Finally, I put it together. Eva Faus's boyfriend.

Just then, Eva herself trots out of the studio. She gives the biker an exasperated look.

"Cisco, you busting Ali's chops?"

A flash of Prussian-blue eyes. "Not me."

"He's an incorrigible flirt, Ali, but completely harmless." Eva punches the biker's arm before she swings a well-muscled leg over the bike. "Paychecks are in. See you in class tomorrow."

I can't help watching the motorcycle weave through traffic. Two blocks up, Cisco takes a right, but not before lifting an arm to wave. It's as if he *knows* I'm following their progress. My cheeks grow warm as I hurry into the studio. What exactly did the dude mean when he said he *pointed* me out to Eva last spring?

A glance at the clock above the counter confirms my suspicion: I have less than five minutes before class starts. I tear into the teachers' dressing room without a word to anyone, change as fast as I can and skid into Studio A just a microsecond before Quentin shuts the door.

Samantha's blue eye is practically green.

"Little Miss Dancergirl," she hisses as we line up at the barre.

"Have you figured out who *shyboy* is?" Keisha whispers. "Because I thought about it. He's probably someone younger. That's why he's afraid to talk to you!"

"There's not really a *shyboy*." Blake laughs. "They're scamming—"

Quentin raps the piano. "I said 'fifth position.' However, if certain *ladies* prefer to chat, the hallway is right outside the door."

Blake's face turns so red you'd think it was a piece of raw carne. He shoots me a look like it's all my fault before he moves away. It reminds me of Jacy barreling into the street and then turning on me after I yelled at him. Which seems like the start of all my problems with him. Or maybe *his* problems with me. My breath quickens. How could he not tell me he's at that private school—

Quentin raps on the front mirror. I look up, startled. I'd completely forgotten where I was.

"All right, luvies. Eyes on me!"

As soon as I get out of Moving Arts, I call Clarissa.

"That dude on the bike sounds pretty cool," she informs me.

"I don't know. He's a lot older."

"But cute."

"In a Hells Angels kind of way. Don't you think it's creepy? Hooking up with the choreography teacher and hitting on her student at the same time? Because he was definitely flirting, despite what Eva thinks. He's seen *dancergirl,* too."

Clarissa laughs. "Everyone's seen *dancergirl.* A hundred thousand views and that's before Charlie uploaded the new one. *First Day of School.* I'll send it to your cell."

"That many hits? They're not *that* good."

"Sure they are! They're going to get you from the back row to center stage, and Charlie into USC film school—or beyond." Clarissa speaks quickly, which she does whenever she gets excited. "But the stuff that Blake kid said means we have to move before people catch on. You need a permanent stylist. I'll talk to Charlie and see what kind of look he wants. I'm thinking kind of retro—" She takes a breath. "Are you stoked?"

"I guess."

I've reached the curve in the street and look up. Like a lighthouse beacon that either beckons—or warns—Jacy's bedroom lamp is on.

I can hear them argue, even though I'm in the living room and Jacy's mom is in his bedroom with the door closed. I tiptoe closer.

"I don't want to see her," Jacy says. "I don't want to see anyone."

"Jacy, don't do this."

When the doorknob turns, I jump back to examine the photos on the wall. Mrs. Strode walks into the room.

"Go on in, Ali," she says cheerily. "He's happy you're here."

Even if she was an Oscar-winning actress, and I wasn't an eavesdropping sneak, the lie wouldn't fly. But I do the same thing she does. Pretend.

"Cool."

Jacy's bedroom is brightly lit. Although his hair is as wild as ever, something is different. It takes a moment before it sinks in.

The room. Jacy's bedroom is always a zoo. Dirty clothes mixed with clean in heaps across the floor. Overflowing garbage can. Stacks of DVDs, notebooks. All kinds of crap piled on the dresser, the desk.

Now everything is neat. Nothing on the floor. Books organized on his shelf. At least two extra lamps.

"I had to clean my room," he mumbles.

"Looks good."

"Yeah. What's up?"

"What's up? I almost went to the FBI to ask them to organize a search party like they did for that Montana teenager. Where've you been for ten days? You never told me you were going on vacation. Plus, Charlie said you left WiHi for a private school." I plop onto his bed. "Is that true?"

He moves to the window and stares at the street. "My dad. He's never liked public schools."

I wait but Jacy doesn't volunteer anything else.

That's it? Dad never liked public schools?

Before I can explode again, a pair of old-school, amber-tinted sunglasses catch my eye. Jacy probably got them at the Shore, not exactly a hotbed of fashion innovation. Or a particularly pleasant place to be when you spend the entire week being pissed off at your father for making you leave high school during junior year.

"Do you hate it?" I ask softly. "Maybe you can convince your dad to let you come back." I put on the sunglasses, hoping to make him laugh. "We all miss you, Jace—"

"School's fantastic. I met a lot of new people, so don't expect a call or anything." When he turns, his cheeks pink up. "And put those glasses down. Who do you think you are?"

"Sorry!" I drop the sunglasses onto the desk.

"I've got homework—so you should go."

"Yeah. Sure," I say.

My eyes sting with tears as I stumble out the door.

chapter ten

"How could I lose her before I even know her? To this dope! This intellectual pea brain! He'll never care about her the way I do. He will never understand her. But here I am, destined to be, forever, *shyboy101*."

The footage is beautiful—Charlie found the first tree in the park to turn completely yellow—and the anguished voice-over is totally believable. Despite his outwardly geeky appearance, he's a much better actor than I realized.

Too bad I can't say the same for Josh. The kissing scene felt *so* awkward. Of course, with Clarissa standing around fixing our hair, and Sonya enlisted to keep people out of the way, it's not like we were in a romantic situation. When we finally moved toward each other for the big smooch, Josh stuck his tongue into my mouth.

"Uggh! What are you doing?" I turned to Charlie standing in the bushes forty feet away. "Sorry."

"Just try again," he shouted.

I gave Josh my sternest look. "Actors don't actually kiss. They brush lips."

"Okay, okay. I get it," Josh mumbled.

"Action!" Charlie called.

Josh moved toward me and we "kissed"—but then I cracked up.

"What now?" Charlie yelled.

"It tickled."

"You told me to brush your lips," Josh said.

"Brush, not sweep with a broom!"

We did the scene several more times. The more we "kissed," the grumpier Sonya got.

"What's wrong with that last one, Charlie? It looked fine!"

Now, as I watch *Park Date* in my bedroom, I wonder if I should talk about Sonya to Josh when she's not around. See what he says. Although honestly, hurt's written all over that one in capital letters. The dude is way too into himself to be a decent boyfriend to anyone. I'd hate to see Sonya's heart permanently tattooed.

I click over to the newest comments on the site. It's hard to get used to complete strangers discussing me.

She's hot
Not. check out the fat ass.
So sick of boring girls tryin to get publicity. she cnat even dance.
dreamed she was my lab partner
Sleep on, chem turd. She's mine.

Weirdest of all, though, are the grown men. I picture Cisco staring at his screen.

forgot how god h.s. chicks r

chapter eleven

I hear the name first. Behind me, in the park. The end of day-light saving time has brought dusk earlier than I expected, so I can't quite see the guy's features. He looks sinister in his long gray trench coat.

"*Dancergirl*—" he starts. The roar of a bus cuts off the rest. I glance at the street. Yes! If I can get to the corner before the bus leaves, I'll be safe.

My legs weigh me down. Heeled boots cover my feet and I can't get any traction. I look over my shoulder. The guy is gaining....

The pneumatic hiss of the closing bus doors gets my attention.

"No!" I wail. "Don't leave! Wait!"

The driver sees me through the side window. Gives an evil smile. A cloud of noxious smoke spurts out of the tailpipe as the bus pulls into traffic. The old man sitting in the backseat looks at me. His toothless grin mouths, "*Dancergirl...*"

I wake up fighting for air. It's 2:00 a.m.

"Mom? You home?" I yell, even though I know she doesn't

get out of work until 6:00. It's just that it feels like someone's in the apartment. Someone who only seconds before stood beside my bed, watching me sleep—

I snap on the light. No one's here.

A metal three-hole punch sits on my desk. It's all I have for protection as I tiptoe into the living room. The apartment is empty, silent except for the occasional creak of a wooden floorboard. I pad into the kitchen. Check the locks on the front door. Everything is exactly the way I left it when I went to bed.

I don't know what I expected. Some *dancergirl* freak sneaking into the apartment in the middle of the night? Mom installed a "guaranteed burglar-proof" lock on the door when we moved in, so it should be impossible for anyone to break in.

Still, I cannot get back to sleep. Every time I close my eyes, that creepy feeling returns.

chapter twelve

In Choreography, everyone warms up on their own. Eva puts on whatever piece of music she feels like and we stretch however we want. She must be feeling particularly nostalgic because today it's the Beatles. "Sgt. Pepper's Lonely Hearts Club Band" segueing into "Norwegian Wood" is like comfort food for a modern dancer. Exactly what I need. I'm so tired from being awake half the night that I thought about skipping class to go home and nap. But then I'd have to answer a million Mom questions. *Why are you home so early? Are you sick? Did something happen at school?* I figured it was easier to go to class.

I'm doing simple stretches, butt firmly on floor. Blake slides over. He tilts his head toward Samantha. She's at the barre, one leg hooked gracefully over the rounded wood. With the other securely on the ground, she pliés over and over, back straight, right arm arched royally over her head.

"Did you hear?" he whispers. "She's got her Juilliard audition next month."

A cloud of fear drifts over my heart. Next year, it'll be me praying night and day just to *get* an audition, never mind actually performing in front of judges.

"I heard her mom's paying Quentin for private coaching," Blake adds. "Rich bitch."

Before I can respond, Eva turns off the music. "Everyone warmed up?" Without waiting for a reply, she nods. "Excellent. Solos are due today so let's not waste time. Who's first?"

Samantha's arm immediately hits the air. "I'll go!" As one, we all turn. She's not only a rich bitch—she's a show-offy one, too.

Sam shrugs defensively. "I just want to get it over with."

"Certainly, Samantha. That's one way to approach it." Eva gives the rest of us a raised eyebrow. "Since no one else is volunteering, the floor is yours. CD?"

CD versus iPod is a huge issue at Moving Arts, although no one in class knows except for Eva and me. For months, the staff lobbied for new sound systems in each of the studios. State-of-the-art docks, better speakers. Just before fall classes started, Lynette called an emergency meeting.

"Enrollment is down, folks. Rent is up. I can either not cut salaries or buy new sound equipment. Your choice."

Which is why Eva's now holding out her hand for Sam's CD.

Blake and the rest of us settle along the back wall. Samantha rustles through her dance bag. She laughs nervously. "It's here somewhere. I'm sure I dropped it in last night...."

"Maybe if you didn't have so many leotards—" Blake snickers. I smack him in the arm. For once, I'm on Sam's side. I'd be a perfect mess, too, if I were about to present.

She waves her arm in triumph. "Here it is, everyone!"

"Oh, goody," Blake mutters. Eva bites her lip as she

drops the CD into the player. I swear she's trying not to laugh.

"Tell me when you're ready to begin, Sam."

Samantha moves stage right. She takes a couple of dramatic breaths and does a few deep pliés before she nods.

The opening bars of a famous piece of classical music catch my attention. I know the name of it but my brain feels like the peas the cafeteria ladies dish out on the hot-lunch line. Soft, mushy and puke-green.

Suddenly, it's Blake who's nudging me. "Wake up. Sam's about to cross in."

I try not to yawn. "Got up early. Couldn't get back to sleep—"

Jacqui, who's taken Choreography for the past two years, leans over to shush me. Sam runs into the center of the room. She flings out her arms and does a strange series of twisting motions, which leads into a sort of hunched arabesque.

It wouldn't have mattered one bit if I'd yawned. Everyone's mouth opens in astonishment. Samantha couldn't have picked a worse piece of music to go with her choreography. Or maybe she just chose awful movements. Either way, the display in front of us is pretty gruesome.

After what seems like an eternity, she freezes. The music, however, keeps playing. Sam looks up. "That's it."

Startled, Eva shuts off the player and begins to applaud. The rest of us eventually follow her lead. Sam takes a graceful, though nervous, bow.

"Comments?" Eva asks.

The hush is epic.

"Then I'll begin," Eva says cheerfully. "It was very brave of you to present first, Samantha. I liked the opening phrase but wondered why you chose that particular piece of music. Perhaps you can tell us what you're going for?"

That's all Sam needs. She starts in about wood nymphs and fauns in the afternoon and the quintessential beauty of the forest—yes, she uses the *q* word. After twenty seconds of her mumbly-gook explanation, I space out. I didn't like her solo but who am I to judge? I haven't even begun mine.

I jerk back to earth when I hear my name.

"Alicia?" Eva asks. "How about you?"

"Oh, uh, it was pretty good. The music was pretty."

Eva looks amused. "It should be. It was written by Claude Debussy. But we've moved on from Samantha. Pay attention, Ali. I asked if you want to present next."

"Sorry. Mine still isn't finished."

Eva runs a hand through her spiky hair. "As long as it's started."

chapter thirteen

Charlie calls during dinner.

"I've got a list of this week's locations," he says. "We just have to figure out when we can meet."

"Hold on." I take the cell into the living room. "I can't do anything for a few days. I'm drowning. There was a choreography solo due today that I haven't even started. And if I tank another math quiz, it's straight to remedial."

"Screw school. This is the big time."

"Yeah, screw school. My mom's going to be thrilled with that attitude."

"Don't you like the new video?" Charlie asks. "My other ideas are even sweeter."

"I'm sure they are, but I need a break. Just a few days. Maybe a week. I couldn't sleep last night—"

"I don't get it! The whole point of being a dancer is so people can see you. I've thrown you hundreds of thousands of views."

"Yeah, but who's doing the viewing? Have you actually read what people write about me?"

"Grow up, Ali. Ignore the things you don't like."

"Sure. You can say that because no one actually *sees* you. No nerdy fan boys discuss your butt. How would you like it if they called you a Tarantino wannabe, with stupid glasses and a pimply face— Omigod. I'm sorry. I didn't mean— It's just weirding me out, Charlie."

"We can't stop now. Please. People suspect it's not real."

"It's not!"

"Just a couple more days and I'll leave you alone," he pleads.

"Alicia!" Mom calls. "Dinner's getting cold."

"Later, Charlie. I've got to go."

I'm pissed off the rest of the evening. At Charlie, for making me feel like a turd. And Jacy, who instead of helping with math like he's done for the past six years, chucked me out of his life for no reason.

He hasn't called, texted or shown up at the apartment since he kicked me out of his room. I haven't done any of it, either—I've got some pride.

Still, I miss him.

After Mom leaves for work, I throw the algebra book at the door. Maybe I can clear my brain by working on Eva's assignment. The rules are: no longer than two minutes, with a tempo contrast and three different directional changes.

After seeing the problems Sam had, there's no way I'm going classical. I choose an old Clash song, sketch the first eight beats in my head and then move to the middle of my room. Last winter, Jacy came up with the brilliant idea of pushing my dresser into the closet so I'd have wall-to-wall floor space in which to practice.

The sequence created in my mind, however, doesn't feel

right when actually danced. I hit Replay, only this time I decide to improvise.

Split leap, plié, half-toe lift. Extend a leg to arabesque, step through lunge to chassé. Not good enough. Start again. Pounding pulse exhorts my body: *Don't think. Mix styles. Take chances.* Hip-hop jump, Martha Graham contraction, grande battement. Change direction. Slow, then quick, quick.

I work until every conscious thought is erased from my brain. I become a true creature of the wild. A faun, not of the afternoon, but of the night. Time stretches, then dissolves....

This is why I dance, Charlie.

Not to count how many views I get on Zube. Or to think about how famous that's supposed to make me. Or even to show off how good I am. For me, it's all about the inside. Dancing fills me up in a way that nothing else does, but it's awfully hard to explain that to anyone.

chapter fourteen

The texts start after midnight Friday night.

Keisha: Wow. Top ten

Josh: You slut!

Clarissa: How could u do this to us?

What's going on? And what on earth did I do to them? Josh, Clarissa and Sonya planned to go to the football game that evening. They weren't at all mad when I told them I needed to work on my solo some more. My friends understand my passion. That's why they're my friends.

And *slut!* What's up with that? I'm about to call Josh when something occurs to me. I recheck Keisha's message. Top ten? The top ten that comes to mind first is the Zube list of featured videos.

The site is bookmarked on my computer so it comes up quickly. I scroll down the day's list. My breath freezes the instant I see the picture. Number seven.

For several moments, all I can do is stare in confusion. It's me all right, but what freaks me out is that I'm not at the park.

Or Sonya's roof—or any other location Charlie shot over the past several weeks. I'm in my bedroom. Alone.

The title of the video taunts me: *Hot Diggity*. Time: 1:08.

My finger has a will of its own. It hits Play. Wearing only a tank top and a pair of old Hello Kitty panties, I dance around the bedroom as if I haven't got a care in the world. After the initial brain freeze, I realize the footage was shot two nights ago. That's when I started the solo. I'd taken off my jeans, but hadn't bothered to put on tights.

The only other thing I know for sure is that it's been edited. Most of the footage is from the end after I went crazy, but the beginning section came from when I first started choreographing.

My face burns hot as a chili pepper. I tap a key and the video cuts off midleap. How the hell did that get taped?

I glance around the room. Besides the bed on the far wall and my desk, there's not much cluttering up the space. The chair I'm sitting in, the bookcase in the corner. There's no camera on any of the shelves. I check the closet. Nothing but clothes.

That's when I feel it. Back of the neck prickle. Goose bumps across the skin.

I whirl. A bloodcurdling scream fills the air.

Sitting on the fire escape, on the other side of the window-pane, is a tiny camera. The lens points straight at me!

For a moment, time stops. There's nobody on the fire escape. Just the camera. It stares at me, I stare at it. Then several things happen at once.

The camera jerks upward. My cell rings but I ignore it. Rushing to the window, I lift the sash and stick my head out. The Minicam is attached to a snakelike cable. I watch in disbelief as the camera rises and then disappears over the building's cornice.

Nobody's on the roof, at least no one that I can see.

I remember the phone. The call I missed was from Jacy.

I hit his number and he answers on the first ring. "You okay? I thought I heard you yell."

I eyeball the floor as if I could see directly into his bedroom. "You can't believe what just happened!"

"Be up in two minutes."

With a click, he's gone.

The doorbell's chime makes me jump even though I expect it. Jacy goes directly to the living room, turning on every light that he passes. The burst of electricity comforts but immediately the vibe turns awkward. Neither of us knows how to begin after not talking all these weeks. But with a quick flick of the WiHi handshake, the moment passes.

"Did the video make you scream?" he asks.

"Who sent you the link?"

He looks uncomfortable. "No one. I was checking to see how many views the others were up to. I don't see why you're so freaked. If you let Charlie shoot it, what did you expect?"

"I didn't—"

"You didn't think he'd put it out on the internet?" Jacy interrupts.

"I didn't let him shoot this one." Miserable, I fold onto the couch and tell him what's been going on.

"Let me get this straight. Charlie wanted to shoot more stuff, you said no, so he goes up to the roof Wednesday night, drops a camera and shoots through your window. Takes a day and half to edit and then, after he uploads the finished piece, decides to do it again tonight." Jacy shakes his head. "What an asshole."

"Tell me about it!" I can feel my cheeks flush all over again at the thought of being half-naked on the net. "How could he embarrass me like that?"

"Let's find out." Jacy pulls out his cell but Charlie doesn't pick up. "Show me where you saw the camera, Ali."

We head into my room. I keep the blinds only partway down to let in daylight. Since the buildings across the street are three stories, not six, it never occurred to me that anyone could see in through the bottom half of the window.

"It was hanging down from the roof. On some kind of cable. But he reeled it up the minute he heard me scream."

"Dude's gone off the deep end," Jacy mutters.

With a vicious tug, he pulls the venetian blinds. The metal slats hit the sill with a bang. The outside world disappears from view.

"Time for a field trip!" he announces.

"To Charlie's?" It's after 1:00 a.m. "Mom'll kill me if she finds out."

"We won't leave the building. You have a flashlight?"

There's one in the kitchen junk drawer. I flick it on. Batteries are good.

Jacy grabs it so I can lock the door on the way out. He marches past both the elevator and the stairwell. Stops in front of a metal door at the end of the hall. Block letters painted across the front announce Roof Access Only.

"What are you doing? There's no way Charlie will still be up there," I say.

"I didn't hear anyone bolting down the building's steps, did you? But even if Charlie's gone, I want to see how he did it.

And he might've left something to prove it's him. You know, in case he denies it."

"Like what? School ID? A note? 'Sorry I'm such a creep. Love, Charlie.'"

Jacy pulls the door open. The narrow stairwell is made of unpainted concrete blocks. From past experience I know there's a filthy hatched skylight at the top of the well. At night, the only illumination filters in from the fluorescent light in the hallway.

Jacy flicks on the flashlight. "I'll go first, then turn and light it for you."

"It's okay. I can see."

I follow him up five steps to a narrow landing. He hits the push bar.

The squishiness of the tar-paper covering the roof is disorienting after the hard concrete of the stairwell. It's actually a bit brighter than I thought it would be. The not-quite-full-moon and distant Manhattan skyline create a hazy semidarkness. I glance at the spot above my apartment, but Charlie isn't stupid.

"Told you nobody'd be here," I say.

No answer. Jacy leans against the open door. Despite the chilly night air, beads of sweat sprout across his forehead. His breath is shallow, the panic in his eyes real.

"Jacy? What's wrong?"

"Can't go any farther," he whispers.

"Why not?"

"I'm afraid of heights," he says.

"Since when?"

Jacy won't look at me. "It's gotten bad lately. I have to do this weather project for school and it's freaking me out."

"Then why bring us up here?"

"I thought the flashlight would make it okay."

"You look terrified. Let's go back."

"No!" He hands me the light. "Check the area above your window. Look for, I don't know, empty beer cans. Carton of takeout. Anything Charlie might have left behind, since he probably had to camp out, waiting for you to dance."

I move toward the edge.

"Be careful!" Jacy shouts.

He doesn't have to tell me twice. The low edge wouldn't stop a soccer ball from falling to the sidewalk.

I find an old antenna, torn clothesline and wire left over from a cable TV installation. Graffiti, spray-painted across the ledge, is a mess of scrawled, ugly lines. A small circle of rocks has some ashes inside.

"Jesus. Looks like either a gang or the local crack den has relocated to our building."

It's bizarre what happens on a roof. But I don't find anything that proves Charlie—or anyone else—spied on me.

When we get back to the sixth floor, Jacy grabs my arm. "You won't tell anyone what just happened, will you? I mean, with me. On the roof."

"'Course not. Lots of people are afraid of heights."

Back in the apartment, my cell buzzes. I glance at the text. "Charlie wants to meet at the Promenade in the morning. Ten o'clock. Will you come with me?"

"Are you kidding?" Jacy says angrily. "Pick you up at 9:30. Can't wait to talk to the douchebag."

After he leaves, I lean against the locked door.

Did Charlie see me naked?

Sick to my stomach, I race into the bathroom. When I'm done, I slip Mom's ratty old bathrobe, hanging on the back of the door, over my sweats. If I had a fur coat, I'd probably put that on, too. Anything to take away the chill that's settling deep into my bones.

chapter fifteen

The Promenade overlooks the river and is one of the most photographed parts of the city. The wide, avenuelike walkway faces both Manhattan's east shore and the Brooklyn Bridge. You can see the Empire State Building, as well as the Statue of Liberty, but neither Jacy nor I are interested in sightseeing.

We arrive first. Jacy had shown up at the apartment wearing a green hoodie and the amber sunglasses. Unnecessary, because the October sky is gray with clouds, but this time I'm smart enough not to say anything.

Charlie enters from the playground end. He's got on a navy-blue peacoat, punched up with a striped yellow-and-maroon scarf. Hard to miss him.

Before I can say a word, Charlie notices me. He shouts from halfway down the Promenade. "You messed everything up! How could you do this to me?"

"Are you kidding? You're the fucking Peeping Tom sicko—"

"You stole my idea. Destroyed it."

"Hold on," Jacy says. "She didn't steal anything."

"Right." Charlie kicks the spiked metal fence that protects people from jumping off the Promenade. "Defend her pathetic, skanky ass."

"You've been spying on me in my bedroom!" I get in his face. "Put practically naked footage of me online—"

"Oh, come on. I did not!"

"I saw the camera, Charlie."

"Oh, yeah? How did I get a camera in your bedroom if you wouldn't let me make another video?"

"Told you he'd try to deny it," Jacy scoffs.

Charlie stares. "You two are insane. If you guys put out another *dancergirl* video, my uncle'll sue you for plagiarism."

He stalks away. I fight back tears of frustration.

"Hold on!" Jacy cries.

Charlie stops but doesn't turn around.

"Are you saying that you didn't shoot the video that went up last night?" Jacy asks.

Now Charlie turns, defiant. "I was in the bleachers, watching the football game with, like, ninety percent of the school. Which you'd know if either of you two losers bothered to show any school spirit. Go ahead. Check the username. It ain't mine."

Charlie's right. The username is *kurvasz99*.

Jacy stares at the blinds covering the window. "He's not lying. He didn't make it."

"He's a much better actor than you think. Anyone can invent a screen name."

"What would he get out of that?" Jacy shakes his head. "It's not him. Plus, he's got a point about the time. The footage was uploaded at 8:26. Kickoff was seven, right?"

"I guess. So who shot it?"

"Question of the day." Jacy picks up the Batman action figure he gave me when I was ten. "Remember when you called Charlie a Peeping Tom? What if you're right? What if some guy spotted you on the street? Recognized you from Zube and followed you home. Dude gets a brilliant idea. 'Why not make a movie myself?' He figures out which window is yours, sneaks into the building. Not very hard. He goes to the roof, lowers the camera and voilà, perv twenty-first-century-style."

"That's disgusting."

"Agreed. We should go to the cops."

I plop onto my bed. "I can't. They'll tell my mom."

"So?"

"So then she finds out about the videos. And sees me drinking. You know as well as I do how she is. I'll be grounded until next summer. I may not even be allowed to dance. I'm serious, Jace. I can't go."

"Fine." He thinks for a moment, and then pulls me off the bed. "I've got another idea!"

By the time we get back outside, the wind has kicked up. Withered leaves crinkle under our shoes like rattling bones. A gull's eerie cry sounds like a woman's scream. The heaviness of the sky does little to cheer me up.

"Where are we going?" I ask.

"You'll see."

He leads me to a brownstone near the end of the block. We climb four limestone steps. The intercom, with its list of tiny-print names, is on Jacy's side of the door. He swivels his head to find the correct button.

"Be right down," a voice squawks through the box.

"Mr. Ryan?" I ask. "What are we doing with him?"

"You know he's a retired cop, right?" He points to the small sign on the inside glass of the front door. "And he's running Neighborhood Watch now."

"How do you know?"

"He and Dad are friends. My father did the nonprofit status for the group, Dad's way of 'contributing to the hood.'" Jacy laughs. "Right after Ryan retired, he got himself elected president and then kicked out all the wimps doing patrol."

I'm still not convinced coming here is a good idea. "You think he'll tell my mom?"

"Nah. He's cool."

The front door swings open. Mr. Ryan is several inches taller than Jacy. That makes the ex-cop over six feet. He wears a faded Henry Street Gym tee. Since I've never seen him in anything other than a collared shirt, it's a surprise to see how massive his muscles are.

"What's up, kids?"

I hesitate. How can I tell a man I barely know that a stranger aimed a camera into my bedroom and put the footage all over the net?

Jacy jumps in. "There's something going on in our building and we want to get your opinion...."

He gives Ryan the SparkNotes version.

"Did you file a report?" he asks.

"Ali doesn't want her mom to know about the videos. You won't tell, will you?"

"I was young once." He shakes his head sympathetically. "And I've talked to your mom. Something of a worrywart."

Jacy gives me a "told you he's cool" nudge.

The ex-cop leans against the rail. "To be honest, filing a

report doesn't matter as much as people think. Everybody wants the police to do something but unless there's proof…"

He sizes up the distraught victim for truthfulness. Distraught victim being me.

"I saw a camera on the fire escape!"

"*I* believe you but…" Mr. Ryan offers a mint from one of those little cases. When Jacy and I refuse, he absentmindedly shakes one out for himself.

"Don't tell us there's nothing you can do," Jacy says. "You're president of Neighborhood Watch, which is supposed to protect the Heights."

"Done your homework, I see." He pops the mint. "Tell you what. I'll sniff around the station. Find out if anyone else has a similar complaint. Check the list of sex offenders, see if one of them has moved into the neighborhood."

"Sex offenders?" I gasp. "Isn't that a little, I don't know…"

"Strong?" Ryan shrugs. "Peeping Toms can be considered felons if they're caught harassing someone and convicted. Doesn't mean they do anything except look."

I doubt the creepy dude will be on any police list. Odds are it's some high school or college *dancergirl* freak looking for publicity.

"Really, I wouldn't worry," Ryan reassures me. "This guy won't be back immediately, if at all."

"How can you be so sure?" I ask.

"Now that he knows you're onto him, it's a good bet he won't return. Last thing guys like this want is trouble. They like easy pickings, not risk. Still, if I find anyone who seems suspicious, I'll alert the patrol cops so they can keep an eye out."

Relief floods through me. "Thank you so much."

"No problem." Mr. Ryan opens the brownstone's glass-fronted door as a crack of thunder sounds. "I'm guessing you two have about three minutes to run on home before getting soaked."

He ducks into his building. Jacy looks at me. "Hey. You're not still freaked out, are you?"

"I don't know. 'Sex offender' sounds pretty scary."

"Yeah, but like Mr. Ryan said, all Peeping Toms do is look. Plus, he's taking care of it—"

A second blast of thunder interrupts. Raindrops as big as gummy bears hit the street.

"Race you!" I dash down Clinton, scoot neatly around a cracked hump in the sidewalk, and don't look back until I'm underneath the awning of our building. When I turn, however, Jacy's not even close.

What a klutz! He's sprawled facedown on the sidewalk, having tripped over the hump. By the time he gets to the stoop, he's completely soaked.

I have the good sense not to say a word. He doesn't, either, just stabs the elevator's five button angrily. When we get to his floor, I hold the door.

"Do you want to come up for hot chocolate in a bit? Mom bought the dark kind you like."

"I've got homework. This new school's kicking my ass."

He walks toward his apartment, head down, as if he's afraid a second crack will rise up to trip him. Goose bumps prickle my arms but it's not because anyone's staring.

Jacy's always been a bit clumsy, but he used to laugh it off. I blame the private school. I'm sure the kids who go there treat anyone new like dirt.

Back in my room, I sign onto YearBook, the high school

friends site. All Jacy ever said about the school was "It's in Manhattan." I type his name. To my surprise, neither Jeremy nor Jacy Strode comes up.

chapter sixteen

On Monday, I barely get to my locker when Valerie Gaines, who works at the school's TV station, materializes. She had to have gotten here early to lie in wait for me. I know that because the *G* set of lockers is in a different hallway than the *R* set.

"Hey, Ali, I want to do a story on *dancergirl* for *Campus News* that could air this week so can I interview you today?" she blurts out in a single breath, as if afraid I'll interrupt before she finishes.

"No."

"But—"

"No!"

"Come on, it's a great story. Everyone knows you're all dance, all the time. But with *Hot Diggity* you're like an internet star—"

I hold my five-pound physics book as if I'm planning to drop it on her toes. "Not interested."

"But this way, you could explain—" She glances at the textbook, gauges the intensity in my eyes and shrugs. "All right. At least let me warn you. Kuperman's test is hard. Our class is two days ahead of yours. There's a bunch of questions on uniform electric fields."

I lower the book and mumble, "Yeah, okay. Thanks for the heads-up."

Val grins. "You didn't hear it from me. And if you change your mind about *Campus News*…"

"You're my gal. Although I won't."

In second period, Clarissa slides a note onto my desk. Now it's Charlie who wants to talk. In the library, during lunch. When I get there, I find him at a table in the empty nonfiction section, a bunch of reference material stacked in front of him. The old-school spy stuff would be funny if it wasn't such a pain.

He shoves a book at me, and then mutters into the one in front of him. "Jacy told me what's going on. I'm sorry I got so mad. I thought he was the one who shot it."

"You thought Jacy did? That's weird. Sorry I blamed you, too." With an anxious tug, I tighten my ponytail. "But already it's out of control. Valerie Gaines wants to interview me for *Campus News*—"

Charlie looks alarmed. "You're not doing it, are you?"

"You think I'm crazy?"

"Good." He lowers his voice even further, which means I have to lean forward to hear what he says. Kind of defeats the purpose of meeting secretly but, hey, it wasn't my idea.

"I figured out a way to make this work," he whispers.

"Make what work?"

"The stalker tape—"

"Who said the guy's a stalker?"

Charlie blinks. "What do you think he is?"

"Peeping Tom."

He shrugs. "If that makes you feel better, sure. Like I said, we can use the peeper to our advantage."

"By taping more *dancergirl* stuff?"

"Shh!" He looks around but nobody's in the library except Mr. May, the librarian with the 1970s sideburns, and he's busy sorting returns. "The bedroom video is at a half-million views. Okay, not that I shot that one, but now that I see what people are into, I've got this great idea for Halloween. Get one of those French-maid costumes—"

"Are you kidding? Some guy you *just called* a stalker spied on me in my bedroom and all you can think about is shooting *more video?*" I stand so fast I knock the chair over. "Great friend you are!"

He reaches for me. "Hey—"

I pull away. "Don't hey me. This is all your fault."

"What's that supposed to mean?"

"Like you can't figure it out. If I'd never agreed to do *dancergirl,* I wouldn't have some crazy pervert after me."

Charlie holds his ground. "Like you said, Ali, you *agreed* to do it. No one forced you."

I dart out of the library without another word and literally run into Sorezzi.

"Yo!" He grabs me so I don't fall.

"Sorry," I mumble.

"Have a fight with the Asian Tarantino?"

"What? Oh."

Charlie stalks out of the library. He looks so angry you'd have to be way more stoned than Sorezzi not to notice.

"Didn't know you had it in you," Sorezzi says.

"Pissing off Charlie? That's easy."

Sorezzi gives me a knowing look. "Not that."

My cheeks grow warm as I realize he's talking about the video. "Listen, Luke, I didn't—"

He puts a finger to my lips, lets it linger. "We could have a lot of fun, StripperGirl."

*Stripper*Girl? Is that what's going around?

The rest of the day is a misery. I was so worried about stalkers and Peeping Toms that I didn't notice the smirky looks people give me. I keep my head down. After the last bell, I scoot out of the building. Skip the studio, slink back home.

"Ali?" Mom's voice echoes out from her bedroom. "Can you come here, please? I want to talk to you."

Uh-oh.

Mom's still in her pj's, hair uncombed. She looks upset.

Cautiously, I sit on her desk chair. "What's up?"

"I want to tell you something."

That's when I realize what's coming. The good news is that it's not about me. The bad news is it'll be some terrible tale about a reckless teenager ending up in the E.R.

Yep. This time, it's a car full of Staten Island kids joyriding on the BQE, "too drunk to put on their seat belts...."

I've heard variations of this story since I was ten. Make that eight.

When she's done painting every gory detail, she wags a finger. "If I ever, and I mean ever, catch you and your friends—"

"Don't say it, okay? No drinking. No getting high. No having fun. Ever. I promise to buckle my seat belt every single day, even though none of my friends have cars. Or licenses. How about if I wear a bike helmet in the subway? There could be a train collision or earthquake or—"

"Watch the attitude," Mom warns. "If you were there—"

"But I wasn't. And I'm never going to be a nurse, so I won't ever have to see a bunch of bloody, half-dead kids—"

"Let's hope not," Mom mutters.

"Can I go now please?"

She holds up a hand. "Wait a sec. Why are you home so early?"

"Headache. And it's not getting any better."

I lie on the bed but the instant my eyes close, my cell rings. Clarissa.

"Just talked to Charlie," she says. "He told me what you said in the library—"

Great. So I'm ruining your future career, too?

"—and I told him what a jerk he is. A real stalker's after you? That's horrible."

"It might not be as bad as it sounds." I explain Ryan's theory and then move on. "Listen, Clarissa, I've got to ask you something. Promise you'll tell the truth!"

"Always do."

I spit out the question. "Is everyone calling me Stripper-Girl?"

"Where'd you get that idea?"

"Sorezzi. I ran into him after I left the library. Tripped right over his feet. It was pretty embarrassing."

"Nobody's calling you StripperGirl—except, I guess, Mr. Too Cool For School." Clarissa sniffs. "I would know if they were. But people are talking. You are so f'ing cool, Ali."

"Hah."

"I mean it. You dance like you don't give a flying taquito what anyone thinks."

"Flying *what?*"

She giggles. "You're just so…*into* it. Half the school wishes they were you, and the other half wishes they loved something as much as you love dance. If you don't believe me, just check the fan site."

"Wait. What?"

"You haven't seen it?" I hear clicking. "Okay, I sent the link. Go in through your computer instead of your phone so you can see it on the whole screen—and then tell me you're not awesome!"

I end the call and move to the computer. Press the Become a Fan of *dancergirl* link that Clarissa sent. The first thing I see is a picture of me on the left side of the page—although I'm not dancing. It's a screen shot someone stole from *Park Date*. Surrounded by yellow leaves, I look into the distance. My eyes are bright, and there's a secretive half smile on my face. I never paid much attention to that section of the video. It's right before Josh showed up. Someone obviously spent a long time choosing the perfect shot—a moment that makes me look, well, desirable. Like someone you'd want to date.

It's weird to think that a stranger went through all the trouble to set up the site. I glance at Information under the picture. There are links to each of the videos and a Where In the World Is Dancergirl? game. Apparently, people are trying to figure out where I live.

I scroll down. The whole thing is kind of funny. In addition to New York, guesses range from Detroit and Chicago to Schenectady. All northern cities. That makes perfect sense because of the autumn leaves—and the rooftop view of the other apartment buildings at Sonya's party. Obviously, I don't live in the farmlands of Iowa.

But then I feel it in my gut. That creepy "someone's watching you" feeling.

It's Brooklyn, all you a-holes, announces someone named

kurvasz. Check out that white speck in the upper left party background. Statue of Lib.

Kurvasz must be the same as *kurvasz99,* he of the bedroom video. And he did more than figure out what city I live in—although he didn't tell anyone the rest of what he found out. He discovered my building, how to get *in* the building, where on the roof he should drop a camera so that it can hang right outside my bedroom window—

I'm about to click off the site, because it's too weird imagining him on his computer while I read his words, but then I get an idea. Maybe *kurvasz* made a mistake.

I click his name. To my bitter disappointment, his home page is blank. No picture—just that shadowy thing the site uses before someone uploads a photo. Since that's how he looks in my mind, even the non-photo photo freaks me out.

He's got no friends, no personal information and only one link: Fan of *dancergirl.*

I click off his page, and then decide to Wiki both *Peeping Tom* and *stalker.*

Mr. Ryan's right. Peeping Toms aren't interested in meeting the people they watch—although stalkers are. In fact, stalkers do weird—and terrible—things if they get mad enough. I can't stop myself from reading—even though I grow more horrified with every word. The Red Dress Stalker made each woman he snatched put on a ruby-colored dress. Then he systematically ripped it to shreds before raping them in the tattered gowns. Another guy enacted some sort of fake Native American ritual before he touched his victim. Satanists, Cabalists…the list goes on and on.

Is *kurvasz* a Peeping Tom like Mr. Ryan thinks? Or does signing up for the fan site mean he's been a stalker all along?

But, really, Peeping Tom, stalker—whatever anyone else wants to call him, it feels exactly the same to me.

With the bitter taste of dread in my mouth, I go to a search box and type *Montana kidnapping.* The girl's still missing. Had she been stalked in the days—and weeks—before she disappeared?

Perhaps it's the Montana girl, or Charlie's ridiculous French-maid idea, but I decide to skip the famous Halloween Parade that zigzags through the streets of Greenwich Village.

"You'll miss the stilt walkers and giant puppets and the bands," Sonya protests. "Remember last year? How much fun we had?"

I do. It was the first time we convinced our parents to let us go by ourselves. But I also haven't forgotten the thousands of people clogging the streets. Hundreds of masks certain to make my skin crawl. Grotesque, hideously ugly or just plain scary.

It's not only that the gruesome disguises and bizarre makeup will give me nightmares for weeks. It's that I won't be able to tell who's behind my back. Staring at me from across the street. Pressed against my side. The thought of standing next to the skeez who's making my life miserable is out of the question.

The night totally blows. Halloween is like Christmas and Mardi Gras and Easter rolled into one. But even when I get pics from Sonya and Clarissa, I don't regret the decision. Feeling sorry for myself is better than *being* sorry. At least that's what I tell myself. Over and over and over again.

chapter seventeen

On Friday, Mom and I head to Baltimore for Tía Teresa's birthday. Last year, we drove down with Andrew in his BMW, the only cool thing about the guy. This time, Mom and I take Amtrak out of Manhattan. I'm nervous the entire trip. Are the glances people give me just regular "check out the kid" looks—or is there something more?

I cower into my hoodie.

Saturday night, the entire family goes to Obrycki's for steamed crabs. Abuela, Tía Teresa, Tío Marcos, my little cousin Maya. I grab a seat facing the wall before anyone else sits. Mom gives me the hairy eyeball but I don't care. If I'm turned away from the center of the restaurant, no stranger can see my face.

Maya has a year's worth of kid jokes saved up. Then Tío Marcos starts in with his. I laugh so hard I practically choke on crabmeat. Before we finish, Mom orders a dozen to take back to Brooklyn.

As we wait at the cash register to pay the bill, a family enters. A sullen girl about thirteen catches my eye.

"Dancergirl?" she shrieks.

I glance at my relatives. Mom's talking to Tío Marcos and isn't paying attention. Tía Teresa and Maya are heading for the bathroom. I motion the girl into the corner.

"You live in Baltimore?" she squeals.

"Just visiting."

"That is *so* cool. Where did you come from?"

I go for the stupid movie cliché. "If I tell you, I'll have to kill you."

The girl watches me for a moment before her smile turns into a disapproving frown. "My friends and I think you're a bitch. You should leave a message for *shyboy,* tell him you want to meet."

She checks me out, top to bottom. It's like I'm on her screen and she can do, and say, anything she wants without worrying about my response.

"You're prettier online, you know. I'm not sure why *shyboy* likes you. Of course, being half-naked helps, but I wouldn't go that far for anyone."

"Ali?" Mom gives me a quizzical look. "We're ready."

I force my lips into a smile. "Well, it's been fun, but I have to go."

Instead of an answer, the girl points her cell at my face and clicks.

When we get back to Tía Teresa's, Abuela brings out her famous coconut-custard pie. We sing a rousing, if off-key, "Happy Birthday." While Teresa opens presents, Tío Marco pushes back the chairs in the living room. The sound of salsa fills the house.

I don't feel like dancing but Maya won't give up.

"Pretty please!" she pleads.

"One song."

We do a semi-okay version. As the music ends, I spin her into the corner. Maya shrieks with glee. "When I'm older I want to be a dancer like Ali. You're going to be a professional dancer, right, like the girls we saw when we visited New York?"

"I'm planning to try!"

Mom smiles. "We're looking at Juilliard later in the year. And some other conservatories on the East Coast."

"Juilliard! *Mija,* that's wonderful," Tía Teresa croons.

"I haven't gotten in yet."

"You will. I know it," Maya says. "And when you're famous, we'll watch you dance on the stage all the time. Right, Mom?"

"Right." Tía Teresa grabs my mother's arm. "But now, Marguerite and I will show you ladies how it's done."

The two of them salsa like pros. I sit on the arm of the couch. Mom's having a ball. She and Teresa dance until they're out of breath. Their hands wave like fans across their faces as they head off to the kitchen for a drink.

Maya tugs my arm. "I'm thirsty, too. Can you get me something?"

I rifle her hair. "Lazybones. It's lucky I like you."

My cousin laughs. She loves when I visit because she knows I'll do anything she wants. When I get to the kitchen, Mom and Tía Teresa are sitting at the table, heads together like they must have done a million times when they were kids.

"One more year and you're free," Teresa says.

Mom laughs. "I don't look at it like that."

"Why not? You'll be able to stop worrying all the time and salsa the night away. Find yourself a good man."

Immediately, I back off. As I reenter, I call out, "Tía Teresa, Maya wants something to drink."

The two sisters look up. I smile brightly, pretending I haven't just heard how I've messed up my mother's life.

chapter eighteen

As soon as we unlock the apartment door late Sunday afternoon, I reach for my cell to call Jacy. Old habits really are hard to break.

"Just got in. Want to come for dinner? Mom bought steamed crabs."

"Mmm. Be up in about an hour."

"Cool!"

I'm sitting at my desk when Jacy sails into the room. "Whatcha doing?"

I blow hair out of my eyes. "Trying to find the derivative of a polynomial."

"Why? Did you lose it?"

"Ha-ha." I close the book. "How was your weekend?"

"Boring." His nose wrinkles. "When did you start getting high in here?"

"Are you crazy?" Quickly, I close the door. "Mom would have my head."

He settles at the foot of my bed, his back to the wall. "Right. You burn incense because you like the way it smells."

"Incense?"

"You don't smell that?" he asks. "Did you go to the woods with your cousin?"

"I didn't go hiking and Mom just did the laundry. Are you saying I stink?"

His cheeks color. "No. It's just— Never mind. How was the weekend?"

"Fine. Except for the fact that I've wrecked my mother's life."

"What's that supposed to mean?"

"Tía Teresa thinks once I'm off to college, Mom can, as you always say, 'seize the moment.' You know, find a man."

"That's ridiculous. Your mother's dated plenty. Andrew and that guy before him—what was his name?"

"Osvaldo."

"See? You're not in her way."

"Except for the fact that Osvaldo broke up with her."

"So? She's the one who dumped that creep Andrew. My point being that you have nothing to do with her obviously complicated love life."

Ugh. I don't exactly want to think about my mother's love life. "And before *that* conversation, I ran into some girl in the crab restaurant who recognized me. She said some pretty mean stuff."

"People are always jealous of somebody else's fame, Ali."

"Clarissa tried to tell me half the people at school want to be me, and the other half wish they had something they care about so much. She neglected to mention the half that thinks I'm a bitch."

Jacy laughs. "No wonder you barely pass math. That's three halves."

I punch his arm. "Let's not talk about this anymore. You never told me about your *Voice* internship. Is it awesome?"

He picks up one of my stuffed animals, a ratty old rabbit, and bends its sole surviving ear. "I never started."

"Your dad! What is with him? He forces you to go to a new school and then won't let you do the internship!"

Jacy tosses the rabbit back onto the pile. "You know the drill. Eleventh grade counts so much, yada, yada, yada."

"Extracurriculars count, too—"

"I don't want to talk about it. I don't want to talk about anything serious. Let's eat crabs, fight over the remote and pretend things are exactly the way they used to be. Before this f'ed-up year ever started."

I grab the Batman action figure. With my best Caped Crusader voice I say, "Don't be sad, Jacy!"

He doesn't even crack a smile, so I toss him the rabbit. "Show me your stuff, One-Ear."

Jacy raises an eyebrow. "How come I have to be the rabbit? I am so clearly the superhero."

"No way! I'm Batman's Queen!"

On the word *queen* I move the action figure's plastic leg and kick the rabbit in the head.

Jacy extends the rabbit's paws. "ZZZZZZAP. You are so lasered!"

The battle is on. By the time Mom calls, "Dinner!" Jacy and I are laughing our heads off. Neither of us notices that poor rabbit's remaining ear hangs by a thread.

chapter nineteen

After Jacy leaves, I check my bulletin board. I'm looking for a picture Sonya took of him and me at Coney Island last year, but what catches my attention is the calendar. A month ago, I scrawled *Baltimore* across the entire weekend, then wrote **★★★*AUDITIONS*★★★** in the Monday box.

First week of November. Time for all good dancers to start working on their holiday shows. All across the country, prancing girls dream of Sugarplum Fairies. Moving Arts, however, does its winter performance differently. Instead of one big extravaganza, each teacher choreographs a piece. Quentin centers his showstopping pas de deux in the middle of a group dance. Lynette always rents Trinity's auditorium. This year, though, she's even more freaked about it. Like at all dance studios, the winter show is a big money-raiser.

"We need to fill every seat," Lynette tells me. "All three performances."

She's so desperate that not only does she raise ticket prices, she offers a set of free lessons for the student who sells the most. Her daily panic makes me knock off "dance school owner" as a career choice.

Audition Monday begins badly. The alarm doesn't go off and I wake up forty-five minutes late. Pissed, I check the clock. It's set to 7:00 p.m., not a.m. How did I manage to do that?

With only fifteen minutes to get ready, I streak into the shower, throw on a tee, blue cardigan, black miniskirt and leggings. Pack my dance bag and hurry downstairs. *Yikes.* The instant I open the lobby door, a cold front hits me. I'm not dressed right but there's no time to change. I skedaddle down the street, dodging the torn newspapers and random bits of garbage the wind whips anxiously about.

At school, I can't think about anything except auditions. It's nerve-wracking to learn a combination in five minutes and try to blow away the choreographer with your brilliance— while everyone else attempts to do the very same thing.

The drama is always high. One person ends up in tears, someone else is guaranteed to storm out and most go home hating themselves, vowing never to dance again. At least until the next day.

During English, I come up with a plan to give myself the best shot at the duet. Directly after school, I volunteer at the reception desk so Lynette can get things ready for auditions. They're scheduled for 7:30—more than an hour after the last class ends. She has to pick up her daughter from day care by six-thirty, so she usually closes for the hour.

"I don't mind staying," I tell her. "Doesn't make sense for me to go home and then turn around and come right back. Plus, you won't have to rush."

She agrees. After she leaves, I print out a sign that says Auditioners—Ring Bell, and lock the front door. I make the bathroom rounds to replace toilet paper, soap and tissues. Then I'm free.

With a flick of a switch, the lights dim in Studio A. There's nothing like warming up in a room with a beautiful oak floor and soft, dreamy lighting. I stretch, do a barre and practice some turns I think Quentin might include.

The wall clock reads 6:55. Still time. I slip my Clash CD into the player. I'd presented the solo before we went to Baltimore; now I have to work on the suggestions Eva and the class gave.

It's heaven to have so much space. A couple of leaps fill the hole in the middle I didn't know what to do with. That leaves the end, which everyone agreed is flat.

I re-cue the music and dance straight through to get the flow, and then keep going. As the music hits its final note, muffled clapping catches my attention.

My scream bounces wildly around the bare room. In the mirror, a man's reflection stares at mine. Cisco! He stands in Studio A's doorway, wearing a black motorcycle jacket. Leather-gloved hands stop midclap.

"Didn't mean to scare you," he says.

"How long have you been here?" My voice wavers.

"Saw most of it. A little rough at the end but the middle rocks. Good music choice."

He steps into the room. I back away.

Cisco frowns. "What's this?"

"How did you get in? I locked the front door."

"I rang the bell but no one answered. Saw the lights on so I tried the back door. It's unlocked, you know."

How long has it been like that? Hours, days, weeks? Anyone could come in, hide in the locker room, attack a Fairy Tale kid, Lynette or me....

Cisco pulls off his gloves. "Seen Eva?"

"Not since class last week."

He leans against the barre. "Me, neither."

"Don't you guys live together?"

"We had a fight."

I pop my disc from the CD player. "What did you do? Cheat on her?"

The vein in Cisco's neck pulses and his face tightens. "You've got quite a mouth."

"Sorry. I didn't mean…"

"I think you did."

"Really—I'm sorry. You just surprised me. I thought I was alone."

"That's what happens when you forget to lock all your doors. Never know who's watching, *dancergirl*."

The phone at the front desk shrieks.

"I've got to get that." I rush past him. At the desk, my voice croaks: "Moving Arts Dance Studio. Alicia speaking."

From the corner of my eye, I watch Cisco leave the same way he came in. The unlocked back exit.

"Sorry—didn't catch that."

I answer the question, then move down the hall. The dead bolt makes a popping sound as I slide the small metal bar across the edge of the door to lock it.

Never know who's watching.

The dread I've managed to smother comes back so hard I'm afraid I'm going to be sick. Before I reach the bathroom, a sharp *bang* startles me. *Now what?* I sneak to the front window, peek through the shade.

"Samantha!" I let her, along with a blast of frigid air, into the studio.

"Where were you? I rang the bell a bunch of times."

"Sorry, I was in the back."

"It's friggin' cold out there."

I don't want to be alone. I follow her into the dressing room. "So. Samantha. Are you nervous?"

She hits me with a suspicious look. "What do you want, LoserGirl?"

"Just being friendly."

Samantha does that arrogant toss of silky hair she's so good at. Before she can respond, however, the doorbell rings. I let in another dancer, then another. The studio fills with worried students, harried teachers. Everyone asks questions.

"Which studio am I scheduled for?"

"What time are the jazz auditions?"

"Do I get to try again if I mess up?"

Lynette finally shows up to organize the chaos, so I'm off the hook. But not for long.

Quentin arrives. He wears a floor-length fur coat that a dozen animals have sacrificed their lives for, but I have to admit he's the only one who looks even halfway warm.

He immediately commandeers Studio A. "Got to be somewhere by nine, luv."

He gives Lynette a European-style double kiss and swishes into the room.

She shrugs. "Make an announcement, will you, Ali?"

Dancers are everywhere, stretching, bending; doing whatever they can to warm up.

"Anyone trying out for Quentin's pas de deux, please move into Studio A," I shout.

"So soon," Samantha groans.

I'm the last to enter. Every girl in the room turns. Narrowed eyes, unfriendly stares. One more person to compete against. Not even Keisha makes room. I'm stuck watching Quentin demonstrate the combination from the far corner.

The duet starts with a sissone, a traveling jump in which the dancer's legs open in the air before landing on both feet. Then the guy pulls the girl into him for a deep lunge.

Quentin demos both parts. Even in my freaked-out state, I can tell the duet rocks. Keisha's mirrored reflection says it clearly. She wants that duet. So does Samantha. I do, too.

I lick my lips nervously. *This* is what's hard for my school friends to understand. It might help to be seen on Zube but only if you have the goods to go with it. No choreographer would risk ruining a piece just because someone's gone viral.

Quentin pairs us up. I'm with Blake, the only dancer taller than me. He's way too nervous to flirt.

"Did you get the count on the lunge?" he asks.

Thankfully, the turns I practiced earlier are in, although we have trouble with the lift.

"Work with my timing," Blake whispers urgently.

Less than ten seconds later, Quentin raps his knuckles on the barre.

"I want full Princess Di, ladies. Up not out." Quentin nods to Keisha and Denny. "Start right of center."

Keisha bites her lip. When Quentin commands, you jump.

Which she does quite well. Samantha's face turns so grim I almost laugh. Keisha's solid performance puts her in the running.

Sam recovers quickly. She takes the floor like true royalty. If she's nervous, I can't tell. Lorenzo, her partner, has gotten a lot better this year. They look good. Every move Sam makes is impossibly extended. Arms float like angel wings.

"See?" Blake whispers. "She anticipated the lift but didn't jump the gun."

Quentin glares at us. "Your turn will come."

Sam and Lorenzo leave the floor. I wipe sweaty palms on my tights. Blake and I take the opening position. As the music begins, I see Cisco in the doorway—but it's only a figment of my imagination.

Instead of a graceful sissone, however, the adrenaline running through my veins causes me to shoot up and away like a frightened rabbit. Surprised, Blake pulls me back for the lunge more violently than he realized. I fly forward, a tad ahead of the beat. That means I have an extra moment to fill, so I arch my back and lean away, as if afraid. Blake has no choice but to go for it. Push pull, pull push—the duet has a far edgier quality than anyone who danced before us.

Quentin looks thoughtful. He switches partners. Blake dances with Samantha, I'm with Denny, Lorenzo is paired with Keisha.

Some of the second duos are better than the first. Sam seems even more elegant, Keisha goes for a perky quality that's adorable. Denny, however, is so much shorter than me that we look ridiculous.

Quentin pops the CD from the player. "Thank you all for an interesting night. List'll be up tomorrow."

He grabs his fur and sashays out of the room.

"Lucky animals," Blake mutters, sweating all over. "At least they're out of their misery."

chapter twenty

Blake's right. Only one thing's worse than auditions: waiting for the cast list to go up. All you can do is second-guess yourself: *I shouldn't have let my nerves get the better of me. I ought to have controlled the arabesque better. Why did I wobble on the turn?*

Jacketless, I throw myself into the bitter wind. Loose garbage lids rattle against the cans. A stray cat meows piteously. A thin woman, face almost entirely wrapped in a wool scarf, nods in miserable silence as she exits the subway—*Fellow traveler of the Yukon, I salute you.*

Clinton Street is vacant, the deli closed for the evening. The only good thing about the arctic weather is that it's impossible for anyone to hang out on a roof. Even Cisco, with his heavy motorcycle jacket and leather gloves, would freeze to death. Perhaps that's why he followed me to the studio where it's nice and warm—if he *did* follow me.

Omigod! Maybe I'm actually paranoid. Truly crazy. Turning an innocent encounter into something…sinister. With my mind spinning, I let myself into the apartment. Take a breath. The smell of bean soup simmering on the stove is the first normal thing I've encountered all day. At the same time, it reminds me I've barely eaten anything since last night. I beep 07 to let Mom know I'm safely in, pop some French bread into the toaster, then check the messages on my cell.

Clarissa: Call me

Clarissa: Where r u?

Clarissa: Call when u get this

Clarissa: Imp. Call!

She picks up on the first ring. "Did you hear?"

"Hear what? I just got home."

"They found the kid," she says.

I set the serving spoon on the counter. "What kid?"

"The girl that went missing in Montana. It's all over the news. You must have heard about her."

"Is she alive?"

"Yes. But it looks like she's in bad shape. They arrested some guy." Clarissa is totally freaked. "There's this list. Any person who's ever been convicted of an actual sex crime with kids is supposed to register their address when they get out of jail. I saw it on the news."

"I know. The police have a copy at the station."

"But here's the thing. You don't have to be a cop to see it. Anyone can check it out online. There are thirty-seven in our zip code, Ali. Thirty-seven registered sex criminals! I keep thinking about the guy who taped you from the window...."

My stomach tightens.

"There's pictures," she tells me. "Sign on and see if you recognize anyone."

"What's the website?"

"Do a Google search for *sexual predators*—I forget what it's called but the list thing should come up."

Clarissa's right. Thirty-seven people on the National Registry Alert list live in our zip. Not only do their names and photos pop up, but addresses, offenses, identifying marks, and aliases are there, too.

My stomach flutter-kicks my ribs. I half expect to see Cisco's face but he's not there. I don't recognize anyone else. They all, however, live in my well-kept and supposedly safe neighborhood.

I click each person's offense. *Lewd or lascivious acts with a child under the age of 14, lewd or lascivious acts with a child 14 or 15, rape by force, annoy or molest children, indecent exposure, kidnapping to commit 261, 286, 288(a),* whatever that means.

Even without understanding it all, it's the sickest thing I've ever read.

Mrs. Strode opens the door in response to my pounding fist. "Ali! Everything all right?"

"I've got to talk to Jacy."

He comes out of the kitchen, chocolate-chip cookie in hand. "It's okay, Mom. We'll go to my room."

I follow him into the bedroom and close the door. "Mr. Ryan was wrong—there are real sex offenders in the Heights. And Cisco broke in to the studio but he's not on the list—"

Jacy pulls me to his bed. "Start from the beginning. Don't skip anything." I take a breath and tell him everything that happened.

He looks confused. "Mr. Ryan doesn't know about the online list? Isn't it the same as the one the cops have?"

I shake my head. "I'm not sure. He never told me about anyone in the neighborhood. I figured it's like doctors. Mom always says that they don't get back to you unless there's bad news. Should we go talk to him?"

"Now?" Jacy asks.

"Yes. I don't want to go by myself and I didn't get his phone number. Stupid."

"I can't."

It's a little after ten, late for a school night, but that's never mattered to either Jacy or his mom.

"Are you grounded?" I ask.

He shrugs.

"What on earth did you do, Strode?"

As if in answer, Jacy's computer beeps. Automatically, I glance at the screen. A tiny picture of a cute girl and a screen name—*quiksilver*—pops up. I'm baaaack.

"Who's *quiksilver?*"

"Nobody you know," Jacy snaps.

Not *"quiksilver's* a girl from school." Or "my long-lost cousin in Vermont."

It doesn't take very long to figure it out. What Jacy didn't say, but probably should have.

Quiksilver's *my girlfriend. That's why I can't go to Ryan's apartment. I'd rather stay here and chat with her.*

chapter twenty-one

On my way to school the next morning, I glance at the deli window. Yes! Mr. Ryan is in the corner booth, eating breakfast by himself. His laptop leans against the napkin dispenser.

He glances up as I approach his table. Politely, he closes his computer. "Don't tell me the guy came back! Because I'm watching the street."

I slide into the opposite seat. "That's not exactly why I'm here. My friend Clarissa discovered a list of sex offenders online. There are thirty-seven in this zip code alone."

Ryan sighs. "Would you like something to eat?"

"No, thanks. I've got school."

He nods. "I'll try to make this quick, then. I was hoping you *wouldn't* see the list, Alicia, for this very reason."

"Because I'd freak? You got that right."

"What you have to understand is that the list, for the most part, is useless." He holds up a hand so I won't interrupt. "Half the people don't really belong there. And the other half are too old to harm anyone."

I slip my messenger bag off my shoulder. "I don't understand."

"Once you're a convicted sex offender, you're on the list. So, let's say you're nineteen and having sex with your seventeen-year-old girlfriend. Then you break up with her, and she presses charges to get back at you. Happens more than you think. So you cop a lesser plea than statutory rape. You never had any intention of hurting anyone, past or future, but still, you're put on the list. Or you got out of jail thirty years ago, and excuse my French, couldn't get it up if your life depended on it. Still, the law is the law. Once on the list, always on the list."

"Most of those people didn't look that old."

Ryan gives me a patient look. "Come on, Alicia. It's not like they update their photos on a regular basis, right? The site uses old booking pictures. I'd venture to guess that very few people actually look like their photos no matter when the picture was taken."

"Then what's the point?"

"Mostly, it's a bone thrown to the public to make them feel safe. I'm sorry, but you want me to tell you the truth, right?"

"Yes."

His eyes flicker toward the window. It's morning rush, and the sidewalk is a beehive of activity. "Have you seen anything else suspicious? Someone following you? A second camera?"

I shake my head.

"See, that's good. And now that we're being honest…"

Immediately, my nerves tingle. "Yes?"

Mr. Ryan takes a sip of coffee. "I didn't want to mention this that afternoon you stopped by with Jacy, but most times a stalker turns out to be an ex-husband or old boyfriend. Obviously, ex-husband doesn't relate to you but…"

"You think *Jacy's* doing this?" My voice comes out an octave higher than usual.

Mr. Ryan's eyes do not leave my face. "What do you think?"

"Not a chance! Besides, he's not an old boyfriend."

"You're together a lot."

"We're friends. That's all. Just friends." I grab my messenger bag. "Sorry to bother you during your breakfast. I have to get to school now."

I hustle outside, shocked at the thought that Mr. Ryan considered Jacy a suspect. Although, after I calm down a bit, I realize it would explain Jacy's secrecy. His moodiness when I'm around. Still…I just can't see it. There's no way Jeremy Carl Strode is spying on me.

But, I can understand how Ryan came up with the idea. The Wiki entry did say there are three kinds of stalkers. The first are the ex-boyfriend types, like Mr. Ryan mentioned. There are also fantasy boyfriends—people who think a random smile or a "hi" at the video counter means you've fallen in love with them. The third type is a stranger who sees you on the street, at a dance concert—or on Zube—and gets fixated. Which means practically anyone in the city could be a suspect.

My cell rings.

"That guy Cisco lives with your choreography teacher, right?" Jacy asks.

It's as if *quiksilver,* and my abrupt departure from his room last night, never happened. I take the hint and don't bring it up. "Yes. At least he lived with Eva until last week. Why?"

"I want to check the registry to see if he's on the list. The names are listed by zip, so all you have to do is find out her address. Can you ask at the studio without it seeming suspicious?"

I consider telling him not to bother, the list is bogus, but then I'd have to bring up the conversation with Mr. Ryan. And when Jacy asks me to tell him everything, which he undoubtedly will, I'd end up blurting out Ryan's Jacy-as-stalker theory.

"I don't have to ask, Jace. Contact info on all the teachers is in Lynette's computer. I can just look it up."

"Is your address there, too?"

My stomach drops. "Yeah."

"What else?"

"Phone number, email—"

"Which means anyone at the studio could have it," he says.

"But only Lynette, me and Mallory, the other receptionist, use the computer."

"Still—if the back door was unlocked last night, it could have been unlocked before. Anyone could sneak in and look up your address. Unless the computer is password protected."

"It's not."

The silence over the phone tells me Jacy thinks that's a really bad thing.

In junior high, being fifteen minutes late was no biggie. At WiHi you have to get a pass from the office if you enter less than a minute after the bell rings. Mrs. Gribaldini, the attendance lady, is proof positive that witches are not an urban legend.

I glance at the bank clock. At this point, there's no way I can get to school on time by taking my usual route. If, however, I cut through the alley behind the large apartment building on Henry, I might be able to make it on time. For the most part, I avoid walking that way because the long row of garbage cans and Dumpsters alongside the building wall smell no matter what the weather. Or maybe the never-ending stink comes from street people peeing in the corner.

The best way through is to take a deep breath right before entering the alley—and make a mad dash. Halfway down, I hear someone yell. When I see who it is, I duck behind a Dumpster. No way do I want to get in the middle of that fight.

It's the neighborhood drunk, or rather, one of the neighborhood drunks. The woman. She's got dark frizzy hair that makes her look like a werewolf with a bad perm. She claws through a garbage can, screaming at a skinny man whose back is toward me.

"You had no right to do that. I paid good money for that liquor—"

"You promised, Mom." Long, thin hands swing the woman from the can. Now it's the guy who's facing me. Luke Sorezzi. Only he doesn't look at all cool. He looks furious. And hurt.

I should have backed out of the alley as soon as I heard them. But now I can't move because Luke will see me. I'm stuck listening to the rest of the awful argument. Finally, Mrs. Sorezzi collapses in tears and tells Luke she's sorry, she won't do it again, and yes, she'll find an AA meeting as soon as he goes to school….

Even I don't believe her and I haven't heard the promise a million times. But Luke's voice betrays his willingness to grasp at any straw he can.

"You swear?"

His mom sways. "Pinkie swear."

Like little kids, the two cross fingers.

"Go on," Mrs. Sorezzi tells him. "You'll be late for school."

That's an understatement. First bell rang at least twenty minutes ago.

The instant Sorezzi is out of sight, I reverse and exit the way I came in. I cannot bring myself to pass his mom. Already, she's back to pawing through the trash, pinkie promise completely forgotten.

chapter twenty-two

Although Luke took the shortcut and I walked the long way, I run into him in the crowded attendance office. He must have stopped to toke up because I can smell the weed on him. Ironic, considering the morning's events. On the other hand, I'm pretty sure he'd say he just needed to relax a little.

He's back to cool. Gives me his smirky smile. "Up late last night, StripperGirl?"

Unbelievable! I could cut him down with one simple question: *Isn't that drunkard I saw pawing through the trash related to you?* Before I open my mouth, however, something changes. Maybe Luke sees the fury in my eyes—or maybe he has some kind of sixth sense about what I'm going to say.

He holds up a hand. "Sorry. I can be an idiot sometimes. You prefer *dancergirl*."

"Actually, I'd rather go by my real name."

He laughs. "Done! Alicia Ruffino, would you go to the movies with me?"

I blink. "What?"

"The movies? You heard of them, right? Or do you only dance? We could go to a club I know—"

I shake my head. He lowers his to mine. "I could get you a fake ID if that's the problem. No worries."

"I don't know, Luke. I'm kind of busy right now. You know, school stuff. And I've got to fix my choreography solo because the end doesn't work..." I realized he has no idea what I'm babbling about. Luckily, I'm saved from my own idiocy by Mrs. Gribaldini's shout.

"Next!" The jelly-roll fat lines around her neck wriggle as she glances up. "Luke Sorezzi, what a surprise. What's the excuse today? Cat ate your socks?"

He leans jauntily over the counter. "Dog, Mrs. Gribaldini. Got a hungry pooch at home."

"Don't suppose you also got a note."

"That would be a no. Same hungry animal."

She cups her pudgy fingers around her mouth as if to whisper. But it has the opposite effect. The Megaphone Voice. Everyone in the room hears her loud and clear.

"What with all the lateness and unexcused absences, you're heading straight toward the legal limit, Mr. Sorezzi. Fair warning—if that happens, I call the truant officer and you might have to repeat eleventh grade."

Ouch!

Luke sticks out his hand, takes the pass and exits without a glance at anyone. Including me.

"Next," Mrs. Gribaldini yells. I move to the counter. "Name?"

"Alicia Ruffino."

She extends a hand. "Excuse?"

"Um, I had to see someone. About, um, a problem."

Now she gives me the jelly-roll neck shake. "You still got

to bring a note. Even if it's a female problem." Mrs. Gribaldini brings up the fingers. Megaphone Voice blares. "Next month, take a Midol like the rest of the girls and get here on time." I feel my cheeks flush as she hands me a pass. "It's going down as unexcused. Next."

I flee. Head down, completely mortified. Behind me, someone snickers. I can practically read the note on the fan site. Breaking news: dancergirl's on the rag. Ha-ha.

Ha-ha, indeed.

Later that afternoon, the studio is surprisingly busy. Young kids, mothers and nannies mill about. They check the lost-and-found box, stand in line. The January schedule has just come out. Lynette, alone at the front desk, issues class cards and collects payments as fast as she can.

In addition, auditioners from last night trickle in to see if the cast list is posted.

How could I forget? I start toward the bulletin board, heart thumping with anxiety. *Could I possibly have gotten the duet?*

One of the Fairy Tale kids streaks out of the bathroom, TP stuck to her foot. "Lynette! The toilet won't stop. Water's pouring over the top."

Lynette groans. "Ali! Would you mind handling the desk for a minute?"

Instead of telling her the truth, *Yes. I would,* I take Lynette's place. "Go!"

She hurries into the bathroom.

"Who's next?"

With one part of my mind, I do registration. With the other, I realize I have a golden opportunity to check the computer without anyone knowing.

The instant there's a lull, I click Lynette's address book.

Scroll to Faus—and discover that Eva lives in Red Hook, near the waterfront. Tenement buildings, low-income housing and old factories rehabbed into artist lofts.

The telephone interrupts my snooping. "Moving Arts Dance Studio. Alicia speaking."

"Hey, Ali, it's Eva."

Yikes. Does the woman have ESP?

"How did you do last night?" she asks.

"What?"

"The list."

Eva truly has psychic power if she knows I saw the registry.

She laughs. "Don't tell me you're at the studio and didn't check the cast list."

"I didn't check the cast list. Lynette had an emergency and I haven't left the desk since the moment I came in."

"You're a better person than I am. I would run to that list even if my own mother needed help. Anyway, I've decided which choreography pieces I want in the show. Will you post? I won't be in until tomorrow."

Lynette keeps pens in the first drawer. "Go ahead."

"Glen's duet," Eva says. "Jacqui's trio—"

"Nice. I really like that one."

"And your solo," she says.

"Really?" My stomach tightens. "I don't know, Eva. The ending's not any good."

"You've got several weeks to fix it."

Lynette taps my shoulder. "I'll take over. I have to call the plumber. Landlord wants me out so he can raise the rent even further, won't fix a single thing…"

I gladly hand desk duties over to Lynette and head down the hallway with Eva's list. At least five students crowd the board. Necks crane upward, eyes scan a printed sheet. A disappointed moan comes from someone, juxtaposed against a happy cry.

Tall as I am, I'm able to see above their heads. Samantha's name jumps out at me. And Blake's.

Just as I thought, the duet was Sam's to lose. Obviously, it didn't matter what anyone did last night, so why did Quentin make us go through the hassle of auditions?

He named me to the ensemble, along with Keisha, Lorenzo, Denny and Riya Stirb—the usual suspects. I text Jacy.

Me: Eva at 612 Van Brunt St.

Jacy: Got it

Me: She gave me choreography solo.

Jacy: Awsm

I'm not so sure. At this point, I'd much rather work with someone than dance alone. I've had more than enough of that.

chapter twenty-three

By the time I get home, Jacy checked not only the Red Hook zip, but also most of the zips in the city. Cisco didn't appear on any list.

We sit in his living room, decorated completely differently from the scruffy Ruffino look. Mrs. Strode went contemporary: chrome-and-leather couches, abstract art, geometric area rug. The ultra-thin TV hanging on the wall fits right in.

"The registry doesn't mean all that much," I say lightly. "Cisco might not be his real name. It could be some kind of biker tag. Or he could have been released from prison in another state and moved here without telling anyone. That's what happened with the Montana guy."

Jacy looks surprised.

"I watched the eleven-o'clock news last night," I say. "I've been thinking about how stupid this list is in the first place. Besides the fact that half the guys are older than your grandfather, it depends on a bunch of lowlifes to actually follow the rules and sign up. I mean, half the kids at school don't do what they're supposed to and they're not even criminals."

Jacy grabs a handful of M&M's from the coffee table. "Well, yeah, I guess. And it's not like you have proof Cisco did anything."

"I know." I tap my foot restlessly. "It's probably not him. But when you're alone in a building and someone sneaks in and acts all creepy, it makes you suspicious. It was scary, Jacy. *He* was scary."

"You just have to be more careful. Check the back door whenever you're at the desk. Don't assume Lynette's done it. And never, ever get caught alone with the guy." Jacy nudges me in a not-so-subtle attempt to change the subject. "Show me your dance."

"Heck no! It's not finished." I make a face. "Even Cisco said the ending's rough. That's what I was working on when he showed up."

"Everybody's a critic. All right. You can show me when it's done."

"Don't you want to be surprised?"

He shuts his computer, peers into my messenger bag. "Need help with algebra?"

"Don't tell me you're not coming to the concert! I'm planning to ask Clarissa if she'll make the costume. You have to see that at least."

"I don't have to do anything!"

He glares at me. I glare back. Honestly. One minute Jacy's a superspy, checking zip codes in the National Registry. With the next tick of the clock, I'm the last person on earth he wants to be with.

I sling the messenger bag over my shoulder. "For your information, Strode, I am Mr. Han's student of the month!"

Right. A couple of hours later, I'm sweating the homework and cursing myself for being so stubborn. If I'd taken

Jacy's offer, I'd be done with this crap. When my cell rings, I glance at the readout. Pray it's Strode calling to tell me "of course I'll go to the concert" and begging me to come back downstairs so he can save my algebra-hating butt.

No such luck. The number is totally unfamiliar.

"Hello?" I say cautiously, half expecting a *dancergirl* freak on the other end.

"Hey, Alicia Ruffino."

"Luke? How did you get my number?"

He laughs. "You're on the WiHi class list."

I'd forgotten about that. Now I'll have to ask Jelly Roll Gribaldini in the attendance office to change my listing to "do not publish."

"Did you think about which flick you want to see?" He laughs in that lazy, stoned way of his. "Or are we clubbing?"

"I don't know—" As I shift, uncomfortable, the math book falls from my lap. Although I stare at the cover, what I see is Jacy and *quiksilver* chatting on the computer. And hear something he's said a hundred times: seize the moment.

"Let's do it," I tell Luke. "We just have to work out a time."

chapter twenty-four

Eva and I are alone in the studio. She'd agreed to stay after class to go over the choreography in my solo. She watches silently, and then chooses her words carefully.

"It seems so much more…pulled back than when you first brought it in, Ali."

I uncap my water bottle. "Not sure I know what you mean."

"Fair enough." Eva thinks for a moment. "Here's a specific example. What happened to the split leap? I remember that specifically and it worked really well. You had that nice, big extension and now you've replaced it with a perfectly executed, but boring, glide."

I can't meet her eyes. "I wasn't sure I could make it every time."

Eva snorts. "Of course you can. You asked for my help, Ali, so here it is. The choreography's gotten too closed off, too internal. Be bold. Go beyond what you know you're good at."

"Fine. I'll put the split leap back in."

"Excellent. In fact, I'd love to see you be more aggressive

with the entire piece." She gives me a sidelong glance. "It's almost as if you're afraid to get out there and really perform."

"I'm not," I say defensively. "It's just…I think the real problem is the ending. It's never worked, no matter what I try."

She moves to the CD player. "What do you want to say? Not just at the end, but with the whole piece."

"I don't know. I haven't really thought about it."

"You chose the song for a reason." Eva holds up a hand. "I know. The assignment said a tempo change somewhere in the music, but that was a nudge. There are a million tunes with time changes but you picked this one. Why?"

"I like it. Isn't that enough?"

She shakes her head. "You need to dig deeper, know *why* you like it. Is it the way the bass line sneaks in and out that turns you on? The dissonance of the chorus, the words? Making a dance is about taking what's unseen in the world and giving it form. It's not about pretty steps."

"I thought it was."

Eva laughs. "The piece doesn't have to end nicely, either. Life isn't pretty—why should every dance be?"

"Quentin's always are."

"Ahh. Then perhaps Quentin is making a specific statement."

I think about the fact that he chose Samantha for the duet. Either Sam really is a better dancer than anyone else—which could be—or the Cranky Brit was looking for something the rest of us couldn't give.

Eva presses me. "What feeling do his dances trigger in the audience? In you?"

I shrug. "They look good. They look perfect."

She stretches a graceful arm. "Would it make a difference if I told you that AIDS decimated the dance companies of the eighties? The love of Quentin's life was one of the first people to die. Most of his close friends followed soon after."

"That's awful! My mother's first nursing job was at an AIDS clinic. She told me that seeing all those young men suffer was the hardest thing she's ever had to do. After a couple of years, she couldn't go to one more funeral, so she quit."

"Quentin expected to be dead by now, too, but he got lucky." Eva reties the sweater around her waist. "We all have more inside us than we're willing to share. Sometimes it's heartbreak, or fear, that drives us to reach our potential."

I nod as if I understand but, really, I don't. If Quentin is so full of heartbreak, why aren't his dances sad?

Eva grabs her music case. "We're out of here."

"I thought you were going to help with my piece."

"I just did."

I follow her into the teachers' changing room. Ever since the camera on the fire escape, I've been fanatical about not changing if anyone is in the room. Slowly, I work my lock.

"Can you move a little faster?" Eva asks. "We need to leave together so I can lock up."

"I usually throw my clothes over the leotard." I try to sound nonchalant. "Saves time."

"It'll take me a little longer but not much."

I slip my cords off the hook. As I slide them over the tights, I realize this is the perfect opportunity to ask the questions I've wondered about for days. But what, exactly, do I say?

Did you and Cisco fight because you found out he's a pervert? Did you move out because you're afraid of him? Is he stalking me?

"Ready, Ali? I've got someplace to be."

I slam my locker shut. "Sorry. I was thinking."

"Always a good sign." Eva pulls on a rainbow-colored cap

and matching mittens. Cold weather brings out the ski bunny in everyone. "We're out of here."

We shut off lights as we go. Eva locks the front door behind us as I surreptitiously check for strangers. No one's watching.

"Doing anything special over Christmas vacation?" she asks.

"Nah. Mom works most of it—extra pay. What about you?"

She gives an impish smile. "Visiting my folks in Florida. Miami Beach."

"Nice! Is Cisco going?"

"He has to work," she says.

I can't read anything into it. Can't tell if they've gotten back together or broken up permanently. At the subway station, we part. Eva skips lightly down the stairs and I hurry across Montague to Clinton.

Francis Whatever, the bodybuilder, is at his window, working out. He winks at me from underneath his barbell. Is that his version of a friendly hello, or a hint that Mr. Ryan put him on Neighborhood Watch duty? At first, I'm relieved. But as I feel his eyes on my back, I wonder if Francis has fantasy-boyfriend complex.

I can't help glancing over my shoulder. Now, he's out from underneath the barbell, toweling off. Oh, God. At least that's what I hope he's doing.

I scurry home. It's not until I'm behind the apartment's locked door that I can relax. I'd called Mom after Choreography to tell her that Eva and I were staying late, so I know she put a covered plate in the fridge. I stick the dinner in the microwave. After it's heated, I find myself picking at the pork chop, forcing myself *not* to think about stalkers. Instead, I go over the conversation with Eva. Quentin never says anything to Samantha during rehearsals except "Shift all the weight to the back leg before you kick" or "Tilt your head more during the chassé." Nothing about what the dance means—to him or anyone else.

Obviously, I don't get it. So I do what I always do when I don't understand something. Call Jacy.

"Is it important?" He sighs.

"Not really."

"Okay. Talk to you tomorrow."

I toss the phone onto the table. Honestly, how much do I miss my old life? When Jacy's humongous intelligence burned through whatever crisis I had—and a chick named *quiksilver* wasn't important enough to blow me off.

The good old days. I could walk home after rehearsal without looking over my shoulder every two seconds. The only people who recognized me were my friends—and no one got mad if I didn't do exactly what they wanted.

Eva's right. Life sucks. For most people. That poor girl in Montana. Quentin's friends, dead of AIDS. Terrorist attacks, hurricanes, oil spills, car accidents on the BQE. All the things that appear out of the blue to wreck lives.

I put my dish in the sink. It doesn't matter whether or not I understand Quentin's dances. I've finally figured out what I have to do. If Eva wants aggression, I can certainly give it to her. Just not the way she's expecting.

The solo's end should shock. The audience needs to feel outrage, confusion, dread. The helplessness, and frustration, of not being able to change anything.

Everything I feel.

Half an hour later, I think I've got it. I re-cue the music to run through one last time. Just before I press Play, a door squeaks. At least I think I hear a squeak.

"Mom? That you?"

I grab the hole punch—*got to get a baseball bat*—and tiptoe to my bedroom door. No one's in the living room. The front door is closed. Everything is exactly the way it was an hour ago.

I really am going nuts—

The scream comes before I realize I've opened my mouth. A man has stepped out of my mom's room. I raise the metal thing in my hand.

He startles. "Ali—"

"Andrew! What are you doing here?"

The guy's balder, and chubbier, than the last time I saw him. "Sorry I scared you. I knocked on the door but no one answered. I figured you were asleep." He holds up a man's jacket. "I left this in your mom's closet. Didn't want to come by when she was here."

My heart has almost, but not quite, quit trying to claw through my ribs. I take deep breaths. I didn't hear him knock.

"How is she?" Andrew asks. "Your mom, I mean."

"She's fine. We're both fine."

With a move that he probably practiced in front of a mirror a million times because he thinks it's macho-cool, Andrew flings the jacket over one shoulder. "I'm glad I got a chance to see you, Ali. You look good."

"What's that supposed to mean?"

Honestly! Does every guy living in Brooklyn have to be a sleazeball? It's no wonder my mom can't find anyone even halfway decent to hook up with.

He shrugs. "Just that you're all grown up. You look more like your mother every day."

I roll my eyes and stomp to the front door. "You should go. Right this second."

Andrew sidles past. Before he gets too far, I extend my hand. "Keys?"

He won't look at me directly as he reaches into his pocket and hands over his set.

"Don't come back, okay? Because Mom's not going to be the least bit happy when she finds out about this!"

chapter twenty-five

The apartment phone rings at 11:35 p.m. I'm on the couch, eating ice cream, watching the cheapo sci-fi channel. I've seen this unintentionally hilarious swamp-monster-eats-virgin flick before but after everything that happened—walking past Francis's window, finally finishing the solo, Andrew's "visit"—I'm too wired to go to bed. Without thinking, I grab the phone.

"Hello." No response. "Hello?"

All I hear is breathing. I slam the receiver so hard, it's a wonder it doesn't crack.

Someone dialed the wrong number and didn't want to admit it.

Yeah, right.

Funny thing about breathing. It's not distinctive the way a voice is, unless it wheezes. And the person breathing into the phone didn't wheeze.

Ringgg!

My heart pounds like a punk-band drummer. This time I check the readout. Private Number. The machine beeps its message signal and I hear a whisper: *"I know you're there…."*

The whispered voice is male. It feels…familiar somehow. That's when what Mr. Ryan wanted me to understand hits home…the shock of recognition blasts into my heart. It's not Francis, not a *dancergirl* freak, not Cisco.

The Strodes have an unlisted apartment number. Jacy would use the landline because his cell would show on the readout. He's too smart for that mistake.

Like the final step in a dance, Jacy as stalker really does explain an awful lot. His weird behavior. The ability to access the roof so he could drop a camera in front of my bedroom window. Knowing when I'm home and when I'm not.

I punch my cell and start yelling before he barely even says hello.

"I'm coming down. And you better open the door. Otherwise, I'll pound so hard, it'll wake not only your parents, but every person in this building!"

chapter twenty-six

Jacy waits in the open doorway of his apartment. He has on a pair of torn jeans and a wrinkled, dirty shirt.

"What's wrong?"

"Not here," I warn. "Not unless you want your folks to know what you're doing."

I charge into his bedroom.

"What am I doing?" Jacy asks.

I pull open his closet door. "Where's the camera?"

"Camera?" For perhaps the first time in his life, Jacy is slow on the uptake. "Ali, you've gone completely schizoid."

"Yeah. I'm the crazy one. Which extension did you use? Your dad's line?"

Jacy's eyes narrow. "Do you want to tell me what's wrong or do you want to play twenty— Omigod! You think I'm the person who shot the video—"

"Took me long enough. You've been screwing with me the whole time. The roof! 'Oh, I'm afraid of heights.' Hell no. You were up there with the camera when I started screaming. That's why you got to me so fast. And that whole show of checking the registry for Cisco's name. Bet you had a good laugh when I told you about him."

"Why would I stalk you?"

"How should I know? You've been weird ever since you left for that rich-kid private school. Is it some kind of hazing ritual? Stalk an unsuspecting girl and join Skull and Bones?"

Jacy walks toward me.

"Don't touch me, you friggin' creep. Even Mr. Ryan knows you're stalking me."

"Unbelievable!" Jacy moves past me to his window. He stares at the street below.

"He tried to tell me but I was too stupid to listen."

Night has transformed the glass into a mirror. The reflection that stares back has tears running down its cheeks.

Uh-oh. I have this premonition. Like something awful is about to occur.

"Jace...?"

"Retinitis pigmentosa," he says.

In a million years I couldn't have guessed that would be his response. Whatever *that* is. "Excuse me?"

"Retinitis Pigmentosa. RP, for those of us lucky enough to be in the know."

"What are you talking about?" My stomach drops into my knees. As usual, my body gets it before my brain.

"It's a disease. Means I'm losing peripheral *and* night vision. It's why I don't go to WiHi anymore. That fancy private school you're so hot about? McAllister Institute."

My throat tightens. "Are you...?"

"Dying?" He spits the word out. "I wish I was. My life is over. I'll never be able to get a driver's license. Never find a decent job. The reason I canned the *Voice* internship has nothing to do with my father. It's just—why the fuck should

I bother?" He kicks one of the standing lamps. "I couldn't stalk you at night even if I wanted to. I can barely see anything once the sun sets."

"What about glasses?"

Jacy's laugh has an insane edge. "That's the irony. Middle finger of God. Cosmic joke." He slams the wall. "The part that still sees has perfect vision. But *that* part's going to get smaller and smaller until…"

My legs can't hold me up. I sink onto his bed. "God, Jace. I am so sorry."

His body is tight, angry. "You can't tell anyone." His voice—and my heart—break at the very same moment. "Not Sonya or Charlie—or anybody."

I need air. As soon as I get upstairs, I lift the living room window as high as it'll go. It shocks me that the brownstones across the street are the same three stories as yesterday. The traffic light blinks the same pattern. Green, yellow, red. Green, yellow—

Pink. I remember the roses that Jacy, Clarissa and Sonya gave me opening night of the spring concert. They were a delicate, cherry-blossom pink. Clarissa presented the bouquet but it was obvious Jacy chose it. He knows roses are my favorite.

Later, we walked to Josh's. His parents were at the opera, and the party was *on*. Pulsing music. Smuggled-in beer. High on performance energy, I snagged Jacy and insisted he dance. When he caught his foot on a stool, everyone assumed he was drunk.

Tripping downstairs. Getting clobbered by a beach ball. Stepping into the street without seeing a car coming. How long had he known something was wrong?

The night his mom cried. The week he disappeared. That's when they found out for sure, he told me. His dad insisted they fly to Minneapolis to see another specialist.

It's why he won't come to my dance concert. He hasn't been out of the building at night since August. He'd have to use a cane if he wants to go himself, and he refuses.

I'm the stupidest, most awful person alive. How could I have considered, for even one second, that Jacy's a stalker?

My body can't stop shivering. I close the window, shut the blinds and do a Google search for *RP:*

A rare genetic disorder of the retina characterized by night blindness, diminishing peripheral sight and eventual loss of vision.

From Bio, I know that *genetic* means RP isn't catching. The definition also tells me that Jacy's right. Ultimately, he won't be able to see anything. Not even me.

chapter twenty-seven

Apparently the fun-house hall of mirrors that is my life is endless. While I was accusing Jacy of being a stalker, elves, or maybe gremlins, were out slapping Moving Arts Winter Dance Fest posters on telephone poles, in store windows and across the construction barrier at the rehabbed brownstone near school. Seven posters, to be precise, are splattered across the plywood. I count in disbelief—because every one of them has my body, and face, plastered on it.

In Person! Dancergirls and Dancerguys! the poster shouts above the list of performance dates and times.

I'm furious—and horrified—and scared. All at once and all jumbled up so I can't even think straight. The posters on the street make *dancergirl* so very public. It's not some underground Zube thing anymore. Now it's a presence in the adult world. Open for everyone—and anyone—to comment upon. Have an opinion about. Make fun of.

The cafeteria is abuzz when I walk through during lunch. It's been weeks since the last *dancergirl* video went up on Zube—and interest at WiHi died down. At least I thought it did. But now I'm getting the same kind of stares and whispered conversations as I got then.

Clarissa pushes her sandwich aside when she sees me. "Why didn't you tell me you needed your costume for a photo shoot? I would have rushed it."

"It wasn't a photo shoot. Lynette watched a bunch of rehearsals last week and took shots of everyone. I had no idea she'd use one of me."

"You would look so much nicer wearing my costume." Clarissa sniffs. "It's coming out awesome."

"I'm sure it is. Don't be mad, 'Rissa. Please. I had *nothing* to do with this. You've got to believe me."

The instant school is over I go to the studio to call Lynette out. She didn't even ask if she could use the photo. But I forgot it was tech rehearsal until I read the sign on the door: Tech at 3:30. Meet at Trinity. No Costumes.

That means it'll be hard to talk to her. She'll be crazy. Tech rehearsal is all about setting light cues and telling the sound guy which music goes with what dance piece. It takes forever. Lynette also makes sure that no dancer gets too far downstage. Rumor has it that at her first show as studio owner, a whole line of Fairy Tale Dance kids took a collective nosedive right off the edge. It was before my time, and Lynette will never talk about it, but now she insists that every piece is choreographed several feet upstage of the edge. She'll stop the rehearsal dead in its tracks if a dance isn't set right.

The bank clock reads 2:45. On the off chance that Trinity's auditorium is open, I head on over. Not surprisingly, the door is locked. Mostly, I imagine, so Lynette can get ready for the rehearsal in peace because she obviously doesn't ever consider security issues.

Instead of waiting by myself, I return to Montague Street.

I'll need major fortification to get through the afternoon. I order the after-school special at Tony's. When it comes, distracted by attempting to figure out what to say to Lynette, I sprinkle way too many red-pepper flakes on the slice. Blotting it with a napkin, I try not to dwell on the disgusting grease that comes up with the flakes, or the Moving Arts poster which stares at me from the pizzeria's community corkboard. A horrible notion strikes. I scoot over to the stack of copies of the *Voice* in the magazine bin. Just as I feared, Lynette took out an ad the way she did last year. This one's a resizing of the poster into a smaller square. All me. And you can still read every word of the original. If the stalker lives anywhere near the city, he'll know exactly when—and where—I'll be practically every hour during the next weekend.

My appetite gone, I fold the paper plate around the slice. Just before I drop it in the trash, however, I look around. No one is watching, so I snatch the poster off the corkboard, wrap it inside the paper plate and toss the whole greasy mess straight into the can. Stupid, I know, because there are a hundred posters like it—but it makes me feel a tiny bit better.

"Ali! I'm so glad you're on time." Lynette's arms are filled with props. "Can you take these? It's the lollipops for Jazz I."

I grab the bags while she unlocks the door. "Thanks. Put them in the girls' dressing room please—"

"Can I talk to you first?"

Lynette pulls the hat from her head. "Not right now. I spent the entire morning doing lights and the afternoon with the sound guy. I have to—"

"Please. It's important."

She sighs. "Okay. Follow me up to the booth."

Her dancer's body is still in great shape and she takes the back steps two at a time. "I had to give Max a late lunch break—"

"Max?"

"The sound guy. And Fred. You know Fred. He's worked for Trinity for years. He's doing lights again—" Her voice trails off as she opens the door. The small booth has lights and soundboards set up behind a wide glass panel that overlooks both the back of the auditorium and the stage. Several headsets and a walkie-talkie sit on the table beside the cue sheets. Crumpled candy-bar wrappers are evidence that Lynette and the crew spent the entire day working.

"I can't afford a separate follow-spot operator this year so we added more light cues—"

"Lynette! Stop. For a minute, okay?"

She sinks into a swivel chair. "You're right. I've been moving at warp speed since 6:00 a.m. I've got to breathe—"

"Exactly."

Although I planned most of the conversation in my head, I can't quite figure out how to start. In the split second that I use to think, she starts in again. "Wait until you see the lighting for your solo. The opening alone has five cues. I still have to tape the stage so you'll know where the marks are. You have to hit them precisely to get the full effect of each cue."

I shift nervously. "Lynette, that's kind of what I want to talk to you about."

"Your solo? Is something wrong—"

"Nothing's wrong with the solo. It's just, I can't believe the posters!"

She grins. "It wasn't me. It's Cisco. Aren't they great? He's a graphic designer for film, you know. He does the openings. Anyway, he told me if I took the photos, he'd design the poster."

"And you let him use *me?*"

"You don't like the picture? I think you look great. Your battement is perfect. Toes pointed—"

"You didn't ask if I want my face posted everywhere."

Lynette looks confused. "I don't get it—"

"It's embarrassing, okay? And, um, dangerous."

"Dangerous? How could it be—what's really wrong, Ali? Performance nerves? You'll be fine. Everyone gets anxious before a show." She grabs a stack of CDs. "I have to go through the music to double-check the order—"

"You didn't get my permission to use the photo," I say stubbornly.

Lynette bristles. "Actually, I did. When you first signed up to take classes. Every student's parent signs a release. You know that. I keep them in the cabinet."

She's right. I've filed the papers myself but completely forgot about them until now. Still… "Who said you could use all that 'Dancergirl and Dancerguy' stuff?"

"Afraid I'm horning in on your success?" Lynette taps the cue sheets pointedly. "You owe me, Ali. I've let you take classes for free all year. And if we don't sell out, there will be no more Moving Arts." She swivels in the chair, clearly dismissing me. "Please lead a warm-up when we've got critical mass. I'm starting the run-through exactly at 4:00. Oh, and make sure that nothing except water bottles are in that aud. Anyone with sticky drinks or food eats in the lobby. No exceptions."

By 6:00, I'm sick of playing cop. I don't care who's drinking what or where they're snacking on chips. The little kids, at least, are gone. They were the hardest to police. They're not allowed to run around by themselves, so I had to spend the past two hours escorting them back and forth to the lobby and bathrooms.

Exhausted, I slink into the seat next to Blake. "Why wasn't I born rich?"

He looks up from *Ethan Frome*. Apparently, every eleventh-grade English teacher in the state assigned the book during the month of December—the plot nothing but a series of depressing events. I've got twenty pages to slog through, too, when I get home.

"Not rich, starlet. Just famous."

"Don't start. I didn't ask Lynette to put my picture on the poster—"

A chill runs down my back. It's the same sensation of being watched that I've felt so many times before.

"What is it?" Blake asks.

Eva's boyfriend is at the edge of the auditorium, video camera screwed onto a tripod. "What's Cisco doing here?"

Blake shrugs. "My guess is he's watching rehearsal so he'll know how to shoot the actual performance. For the DVD sales to the parents."

"Except the camera isn't focused on the stage. It's focused on me. Us."

I've had it. Like a jack-in-the-box, I pop up. I'm going to talk to Cisco once and for all—

Before I can take a step, however, Blake pulls me back down. "Don't get so upset, Ali. Cisco's adding backstage stuff this year. You know, like the extras in a real DVD, so Lynette can sell even more copies. I overheard her talking about money trouble—"

"I don't care what she's in. I don't want to be photographed, or videotaped, without being asked. I'm sick of it."

"*You* might be, but I don't think you should say anything at the moment."

I turn to face Blake. "Why not?"

"Dude's got a wicked temper. I heard him and Eva behind the studio one day. My dad, a champion brawler from way back, wouldn't have come close to winning that one. Don't know why she stays with him."

"What were they fighting about?"

Blake shrugs. "The usual. She accused him of hooking up with someone. Or maybe he accused her—I'm not sure. I hear enough of that crap at home, so I left quick. The dude's bad news. Don't get him riled up right now, 'k?"

I sink low into the cushioned seat. "It's not just him. Lynette didn't even ask if she could use that photo on the poster. I'm really pissed—"

Blake laughs. "You're not the only one."

I look to where his eyes are focused. "Did Samantha say something to you?"

"Whatever."

"Oh, come on. Now that you and she have the duet, you can't dish? What did she say about me, Blake?"

He remains stubbornly silent. Samantha has finally stopped stretching in the center of the aisle. That meant that for the past two hours everyone had to squeeze *around* her. She catches my look and stalks over.

"What are you staring at, *dancergirl?*" She shifts her gaze to Blake. "You, too, *dancerguy*. How stupid do you feel?"

"Not very." He lifts his arms for a lazy stretch. "I heard the phone at the studio's ringing off the hook with people reserving seats."

That information is new. Then again, I didn't give Lynette much of an opportunity to tell me.

"They're not coming to see you dance, that's for sure," Sam informs him.

"Doesn't matter. They'll see me no matter what they come for. And you. Maybe we'll get reviewed in the paper. How awesome would that be? Really, we should give Ali a big cheer—"

"What on earth for?" Sam blinks rapidly. Her giant eye appears to move at a different rate than the brown one. It's a little disconcerting, to say the least. "The only reason Ali got the solo is so Lynette can publicize it."

"Excuse me! In case you two haven't noticed, I'm sitting right under your noses. For your information, Sam, Lynette had nothing to do with me getting into Choreographer's Showcase. It was Eva's decision."

Samantha laughs. "Believe what you want, Ali. I know for a fact that Lynette asked Eva to give you one of the spots."

"Did not."

"Did, too."

Blake puts up a hand. "Stop it, children. Do I have to separate you two?"

"Can it, Blake. The only reason the great Samantha Warren got the duet is Mommy pays Quentin on the side."

Sam's and Blake's mouths fall open at the same time. "Everyone knows, Sam, so I wouldn't be so quick to throw stones."

With that, I'm in the aisle. I keep my head high and manage to get all the way into a bathroom stall, door locked, before the tears come.

chapter twenty-eight

I'm back on Clinton Street, in the sixth-floor hallway unlocking the apartment door, when my cell rings. "Sorry I didn't beep, Mom. I just this second got home."

"That's not why I'm calling," The wail of an ambulance interrupts so I know she's near the hospital driveway. "I forgot to leave a note. Somebody left a bag for you on the mat in front of the door. I put it on your bed."

"Okay, thanks." I juggle backpack and keys, coat and scarf.

"Long rehearsal?"

"The longest."

"Supper's in the fridge," she tells me.

"Got it. Thanks. Have a good night—"

"Ali? Don't hang up." She pauses to let a truck rattle by. "I'm sorry I'm not there to tell you in person, but I want you to know how proud I am of you."

I sit at the kitchen table. "What did I do?"

"Didn't you see the posters? I went to the market this afternoon and there they were. There you were! I am so excited." She giggles. "I took down a couple when no one was looking.

I hope Lynette won't mind. I'm keeping one and sending the second off to Baltimore. Maya will be *so* excited. How cute is it? 'Dancergirls and Dancerguys.' I wonder how Lynette came up with that idea."

"Mom—" I start, but can't quite bring myself to burst her bubble. "Never mind."

"You don't sound very excited, Ali."

"Just tired. Had to ride herd on the little kids at tech so I didn't get a chance to do my homework."

"Don't stay up too late. You want to be fresh for the performances this weekend. I reserved a ticket for Saturday night *and* the Sunday matinee—" A second ambulance screeches past. Mom sighs. "Gonna be a busy shift. Got to run. 'Night, *mija*."

"'Night, Mom."

Halfway through dinner, I remember the reason Mom actually called. I hurry into my room. Shake the plastic bag. Several pieces of fabric fall onto my bed. My costume! Obviously, Clarissa went home and finished it right after school. She left a note in her distinctive flowery writing. It's a detailed set of instructions explaining how the pieces go.

Clarissa found a bunch of lacy thrift-store skirts. She sewed the tan one into a tight-fitting undershirt. Then she layered one of my old black leotards over it and made a bunch of "artistic" rips so tan lace peeks through black nylon. She sewed two skirts together in a torn, patchworky kind of thing. Then she punked the whole look up with chain belts from the seventies.

Watching myself in the mirror, I try a couple of moves. After seeing how the lights were designed, I'm pretty sure the costume will look great from the stage. If only I felt the same way about the dance. I can't get what Sam said out of my head: *I know for a fact that Lynette asked Eva to give you one of the spots.*

The possibility that it's true hurts more than I could have imagined.

My first thought, as always, is to call Jacy. I resist. If he blows me off, I'll lose it. Instead, I text Clarissa to thank her for the costume.

Call online. Want 2 see how it looks on u comes the reply.

It takes a few moments to set up the laptop so Clarissa can see the whole costume.

"Turn around. Dance a bit." On-screen, she bites her lip. "Do you want me to make the skirt a little shorter?"

"Uh-uh. I like how it swirls."

She grins. "Me, too. I am soooo excited. My first dance costume. You better do good."

"Thanks for the vote of confidence."

"Just kidding. You'll be great, I know it."

"Yeah, well…" I feel myself deflate.

Clarissa catches the change. "What's wrong? More creepy stalker stuff?"

"Not really. But at rehearsal today, Sam told me that I only got the solo because Lynette made Eva give it to me."

Clarissa looks relieved. "That's not so bad."

"Not so bad? Don't you understand? That means I don't deserve it—the solo's not good enough. *I'm* not good enough."

She shakes her head. "You are. At least you are now. Didn't you tell me Eva worked on it with you? She wouldn't let you go onstage looking like a jerk."

"Thanks. Again."

"Stop wallowing, Ali. It's what we told you when it all started. *Dancergirl* is going to help. It's like having a rich father, or an uncle in the business. Neither of which you have, in case you've forgotten that fact. Didn't you tell me that Sam girl's mother pays one of the teachers to coach her? This is your way of evening up the playing field."

"Leveling the playing field," I mumble.

"Whatever. People who have pull get places."

"But—"

"No buts. Think of *dancergirl* like a grandfather in the business. Someone who gives you that extra little edge. You still have to live up to it. And I repeat—Eva would not let you go on if she didn't think you'd do a great job. Just because something else helped you get it doesn't mean you don't deserve it."

chapter twenty-nine

In homeroom Sorezzi stops by my desk. "Text me when you're done with rehearsal."

He called after Clarissa and I spoke last night. I couldn't stall any longer so I said we could hang tonight. Sandwiched between first tech and dress rehearsal, *second* tech almost always goes quickly. The cues are set and it's just a matter of running through.

"Probably be done by six," I tell him.

When I arrive at Trinity, I sneak into an alcove high in the balcony to hide from Lynette and the rest of the dancers. I don't want to get into it with any of them—nor do I want to play babysitter. Plus, I need to use the wait time to get my homework done. Luke wants to go into Manhattan, so I'll be dead tired by the time the day ends.

The solo goes well. I hit the tape marks on the stage, feel the light. When it's over, I slip into jeans, a pullover sweater and jacket. I've also got a green holiday scarf that I picked up at the secondhand store last year. I wrap it around my neck using the jaunty-knot thing Clarissa taught me how to tie and imagine I look quite European.

As I walk down Montague, I keep my head down in the hope that none of my friends will notice me. I haven't told anyone—and I mean *anyone*—that I'm meeting Sorezzi. It was an impulsive yes. Once the night is over, I will have kept my promise to go out and can just move on.

The subway entrance is packed with people coming home after work and I have a hard time finding him.

Someone taps me. "Behind you, Alicia Ruffino."

"Luke!"

He pulls me toward the steps. "Come on. We've got lots to do before your curfew."

I'd told him that I had to be home by nine o'clock. Mom will assume rehearsal ran late so I won't have to get into the fact that I'm leaving Brooklyn on a school night.

We exit the subway at Herald Square and walk to Macy's. The Christmas window displays are always fabulous. Mechanical elves and dolls dressed in old-time costumes move smoothly inside detailed, complicated little Victorian sets. As we wait in the line for our turn to view the displays, I can't help checking over my shoulder. I'm not sure how I think I'll recognize the stalker in the middle of a bunch of tourists but glancing back has become second nature.

"Something wrong?" Luke asks.

I turn to face him. "Crowds freak me out lately."

He laughs. "Don't worry. I won't lose you."

The line inches forward. Luke seems different. The cool 'tude that fits like a second skin has vanished. Eyes wide with excitement, stonerboy actually looks younger. Happier.

"Bet you used to come here with your mom," I say—and

immediately want to kick myself. What a lame, insensitive thing—

Luke smiles. "How'd you know?"

Relieved that he's not insulted, my hand slips into his. "Because I used to come with mine. Back in the day."

"Back in the day," he repeats. Then…silence…as we both remember clasping bigger hands in front of these windows, wondering if we can ever feel that safe again.

After we pass through the line, Luke buys two huge, salted pretzels from the cart on the corner. There's another place he wants to go, but he won't tell me where.

"It's a surprise," he says.

We head uptown, crossing streets and avenues crowded with tourists. The jangle of Salvation Army bell-ringers and a smoky smell fill the air—roasted chestnuts sold by street vendors. Luckily, we have the pretzels to munch as neither of us has much to say.

We pass Rockefeller Center. When I was little, Mom and I always made this our second stop. I tug Luke's arm. "Let's see the tree."

I drag him around the corner so we can enter from Fifth Avenue. Rockefeller Center's east border is directly across from St. Patrick's Cathedral. Huge marble spires and stained-glass windows tower over the entire area. If you enter the plaza from that side, there's an added sense of drama. A row of lit-from-within angels, spun from thick white straw, hold trumpets aloft. The huge creatures beckon.

I hop up to tightrope walk the long granite planter surrounding the angels.

"Follow the leader," I call out.

Luke shakes his head, keeping his feet firmly on the ground. Stonerboy's back but I don't care. I've tightroped that planter since I was been four and I'm not about to stop now.

After I'm done playing circus performer, Luke and I elbow our way through the throng. From the center of the plaza, a large, open square is set several stories below ground level. The famous Christmas tree is as tall as my apartment building. At least that's how it seems. Thousands of colored lights strung along its branches create a magical glow.

"How pretty is that?" I breathe.

Beside the tree, the skating rink shines icy-white. *The Nutcracker* plays through the speakers. I've seen the ballet lots of times with Mom, Maya and Tía Teresa. I hum along happily. It's hard to stay focused on creepoids while listening to "Waltz of the Flowers."

"Coming into Manhattan was an excellent idea," I tell Luke.

On the rink, one man stands out. Trim, not too tall, not too short, starting to go bald—anyplace else he'd blend into the crowd. But out on the ice—he's a star. He wears a red-and-blue snowflake sweater, topped off with a bright red scarf. The ends fly behind him as he whips across the rink. I know *he* knows he's being watched—but he's enjoying it. No, not just enjoying it—he relishes the attention. I remember that feeling. Moving beautifully, in another world, but happy to have the audience *with* you to share the glow. It makes me mad. I haven't had a moment like that since I saw the stupid camera outside my window.

The skater nails a fancy jump, and then takes an easy spin that morphs into a perfect, moving arabesque. Wow! What must *that* feel like? Effortlessly gliding across the ice…

Luke's breath tickles my ear. "Seen enough? We have a few more blocks to go."

At the corner, I take one last, lingering look. This time, it's not because I'm afraid I'm being followed. It's just that I think I was wrong. Maybe the best way to see the angels is from afar. As wonderful white-and-light beings glowing from within. That way, you don't realize they're made from stiff curlicues of straw.

"Can I open my eyes?" I ask. "Please!"

"Ten more seconds."

I am not a happy camper. It's insane to walk through Central Park at night. Yes, there are streetlamps and paved paths but there are also plenty of places for someone to jump out at us. I finger my cell. 505—SOS. I wonder if I can text in the dark.

To make things worse, for the last hundred yards or so, Luke insists I close my eyes as he guides me down a path. Finally, he stops.

"Okay. You can open them now."

It takes a moment to figure out what I'm looking at. "The Carousel?"

He nods. I'm not sure what to say. It's a December weeknight. The thing is capital *C* Closed. How does Sorezzi not know this?

"Sorry to disappoint you but the Carousel never stays open at night. Even in summer." I know this for a fact because I can read the sign: Open Daily. 10:00 a.m. to 6:00 p.m. "It's a nice idea but, really, we should go. My mom would go into cardiac arrest if she knew where I was right now."

"But she doesn't." He dangles a chain.

"What's that?"

"The keys to a ride you'll never forget."

"You have keys to the Carousel? How did you— Did you steal them?"

Luke laughs, not the least bit offended. "No, I did not steal them. I borrowed them. My uncle used to work for Parks and Rec. He moved to Transportation a few years ago, but they never asked for the keys back."

"How do you know they haven't changed the locks?"

Luke gives me a wicked grin. "We'll just have to see, won't we?"

He appears way too confident for the keys not to work. A click at the wrought-iron gate confirms the guess.

I don't want to get into a fight. I also don't want him to think I'm a total wimp but the night has ceased being fun. An image from one of my nightmares is way too present. The guy in the trench coat chasing after me in the park—

"We'll get arrested!" I tell Luke.

"Be brave. I won't turn on the lights. Or the calliope. You'll just have to imagine music while you ride."

"Are you insane? You're going to actually start the thing up?"

He spreads his arms. "We haven't seen a single person since we turned down this path. No one will know. We'll ride for less than three minutes. Two times around, I promise. It'll be awesome. Go choose a horse."

The faster I get on the ride, the faster we go home.

At least fifty stallions are stationed around the platform. Each is unique, specially carved and painted but I'm not picky. I jump to the round, wooden floor and point to the first horse I come to.

"This one."

Luke laughs. "Take your time, why don't you? Okay. Saddle up. I'll get on after I get her going."

He takes a flashlight from his backpack and moves to the control box. Within seconds, the machinery inside the Carousel groans. My horse starts to move. Forward as well as up and down. Luke clambers onto the horse beside me.

"Woo-hooo!" he cries.

The lights of distant skyscrapers twinkle down at us. For maybe a minute, it's truly unbelievable. The single most romantic thing that's ever happened to me. Then I see something. A shadow, darker than the surrounding area, moves under an oak tree. I crane my neck, instantly afraid of what's there—

"Everything okay?" Luke asks.

"I think someone saw us. We should get off, Luke. Please."

He doesn't argue. Less than thirty seconds after Luke jumps off, the Carousel grinds to a halt. I stare at the oak tree. Nobody's watching us; at least no one I can see. Must have been the wind, I tell myself, brushing against the branches....

"Need help getting down?" Luke calls.

"I can do it."

We meet at the gate and he locks it back up.

"That was fun," I lie, "but we've really got to head back to Brooklyn."

"I have one more surprise."

"Luke!"

Honestly. The date that never ends. It might be funny if I wasn't so uncomfortable. Why did I let him drag me into Central Park in the first place?

He seems completely unaware of my semihysterical state. I can't stop shivering. Every tree we come to, I imagine that we'll get jumped. Or My Own Personal Stalker will dash out, smash a rock over Luke's head and steal me away....

An owl hoots. Startled, I look around but can't find either

the bird or another person. Luke is totally calm. He finds a spot on the edge of the meadow next to a group of laurel bushes.

"Why are you stopping?" I ask.

"You'll see." He unzips his backpack, lays out a checkered blanket and unscrews a thermos. A picnic? In December. At night?

Luke pours a steaming drink into the thermos cup. He holds it out with the most innocent of smiles.

"Hot chocolate, *dancergirl?*"

"Is this really just hot chocolate?"

"What do I look like, a drunk?" He smiles, then after a moment pulls out a joint. "Why do you look like that?"

"Like what?"

"Like you just got the extra-credit answer to Kuperman's physics test."

I laugh. "I was wondering how long it'd be before this came out."

After checking one last time to make sure we're not being watched, I give in. Luke and I take turns drinking hot cocoa and passing the j. It's not long before I'm warmed up—and well on my way to getting wasted.

I hold up a hand. "I'm good."

He grins. "So am I."

Luke pinches the j and drops it into his pack. He screws the cup back onto the thermos and tosses that in, too. Using the backpack as a pillow, he stretches out, extending an arm for me. Silently, we stare at the heavens. We're in the center of Manhattan so there aren't any stars, at least none that I can see, but there is a moon. Not quite full, it hangs above us like an enormous Christmas ornament.

"Luke—"

"Shh, don't say anything."

"I have to see what time it is." I pull out my cell. 9:17. "Omigod! I should have been home by now. Mom will flip. I'm supposed to beep her as soon as I get in."

"So? Beep her."

"But I'm not home."

Luke laughs. "She can't see you. What time does your mom get out of work?"

"7:00 a.m. She supervises the night shift at the hospital."

"Excellent. Tell her you're home. She won't know the difference."

This is not right on so many levels. But I can't wait until we get back to Brooklyn to hit the code or she'll send the cops after me. I press 07 for OK.

"Don't tell me you never figured that out before." Luke grins. "Dude, you've got the perfect life."

"Right. Except if something happens and she finds out—"

"She won't find out. Relax." Luke pulls me back down to the blanket. "It's the same as the Carousel. No one'll ever know we've been here."

He shifts so that he's facing me. With an incredibly smooth motion, he leans over to kiss me. It's a little like kissing Josh— kind of sloppy. Unlike Josh, however, Luke immediately starts to grope under my jacket. I push his hand away. He brings it back.

"Come on, Ali," he whispers. "It's not like you haven't done this before."

I pull away. "What's that supposed to mean? Is there some new *dancergirl* rumor going around? A secret video I haven't seen—"

"Not *dancergirl*. Jacy."

"*Jacy?*"

"Yeah. You and Strode had something going on last year for sure. Then, what? He dumped you when he went to private school?"

"No! I mean, he has new friends but so what? It's not like we ever did anything. We're friends—"

Luke shrugs. "Even better. Leaves things open for me—" He tries to pull me next to him but I won't go.

"Unbelievable," I breathe. An idea takes hold and won't let go. "You *planned* this. Did you work it out with Charlie? Or *kurvasz99?*"

"Wha—who?"

Wild, I look round. "You didn't happen to come to this spot. You scouted it out ahead of time—or maybe Charlie did. Yeah, this has Liu written all over it. The locations, the thermos. I bet it's Charlie's uncle who worked for Parks and Rec, not yours." I point to a stand of maples. "Is he filming this with a zoom lens?" I raise my voice. "Come out, come out, wherever you are—"

Luke clasps his hand over my mouth. "Stop! Someone might hear you—"

I struggle to push him away. Luke whispers, frantic. "Please, Ali. I'll let you go but don't scream."

When I nod, he cautiously removes his hand. "Listen—"

"No!" Childishly, I put my hands over my ears, and then take them down. "What are you guys going to call this? Not *Park Date.* Charlie already used that. *Perfect Date?* Yeah, I bet that's it. How far are you supposed to go with me?"

"You're not making sense. How could anyone shoot this? It's dark—"

"I'm sure Charlie figured something out." I shove my green scarf under Luke's nose. "Maybe he's got some kind of night camera. I saw it on TV. It shoots in green, but you can still see everything."

"Ali, I swear, no one is taping this."

A humongous sense of betrayal fills me. "Then it's you!"

"What's me?"

"Took you all this time but you finally got me alone, didn't you? No one around…"

Crazed, I get to my feet and scoot down the path. After a few moments, footsteps follow. When Luke gets close enough, he grabs my arm. "Ali, listen. It's the weed."

That stops me. "What's the weed?"

"This…paranoia. I did not make any kind of deal with Liu. Why would I? I don't even like the dweeb."

That, actually, is the first thing I believe. I've always suspected he had something against Charlie. "But—"

Luke talks to me slowly, cautiously. As if I'm a two-year-old who might throw another tantrum any second. "I brought the good stuff tonight. Most people get really off on it but it makes others totally paranoid. Think everyone's out to get them."

"I know what *paranoid* means," I snap.

Luke tries a laugh. "See, now you think I think you're stupid. I don't. But we should get out of here. You might— Never mind."

"Might what?" I ask. "Never mind what?"

He shoulders his backpack. "Uh-uh. Don't want to give you any more crazy ideas than you already have. Let's get you a water. The worst of it should wear off by the time we hit Brooklyn…."

Neither of us says much the whole way home. I lean against the subway window, pretend to fall asleep. Secretly, I watch the people on the train through half-closed eyelids. No one appears to be following us.

When we get to my building, I refuse to let Luke inside. I don't want him to know which apartment is mine. It's not until later that I realize all he has to do is check the buzzer buttons.

"You sure you're all right?" he asks. "I don't mind staying—"

"That's okay. I'd rather be alone."

He shrugs. "All right but, you know, if you freak again, you can call, or text."

"I've got Jacy. He lives right below me."

Luke's eyes dim. "Right. Strode. Tell him I say yo."

Sorezzi takes the stoop stairs quickly. For a moment, I feel a tinge of…something. Pity? Sadness? I wonder where *his* mom is right now, why she's not worried about him. Is she passed out on the couch in their living room? Sitting on a stool in the old-man bar on Lemon Street? The one that smells like stale beer and cigarettes no matter what time you walk past.

Once inside my apartment, I carefully lock the locks. Then I beep Mom. At the very last second, I remember I've already done that and disconnect. Awkward! I can just imagine the conversation when she called to find out why I double-beeped her.

Just making sure you know I got home. Two hours ago. When I beeped the first time.

Clearly, I am not cut out for a life of crime.

chapter thirty

Just before school the next morning, I check the internet. No
new video. There is, however, a photo on the fan site. The
camera caught me looking down at the skating rink in Rockefeller Center. There's a spotted: dancergirl in NYC caption.
Strange but it doesn't freak me that much. It feels sort of innocent, captured by a *dancergirl* fan who noticed me in the
crowd. Not something stalker-ish.

I shut the laptop and grab my messenger bag. No way do I
want another run-in at the attendance office with Jelly Roll
Gribaldini. A quick double-check to make sure the solo costume is inside the bag before I scurry off. Dress rehearsal's in
the afternoon, opening night on Friday. As if that isn't stressful enough, I have to face Sorezzi in less than half an hour.
What am I going to say? Now that I'm not high, I feel pretty
stupid about the way I acted.

I needn't have worried. Sorezzi's back to pretending I don't
exist. He doesn't glance at me in Homeroom or Physics, the
only class we have together.

Dress rehearsal is a mess. Missing props, lost tights, late entrances. If I were Lynette, I'd be in tears. But she looks quite cheerful.

"Bad dress rehearsal, good opening night," she trills. "I want everyone onstage at 6:00 tomorrow for the group warm-up. Show starts at 7:00 on the dot. Get a good night's sleep, dancers. Ali, did you give out the tickets?"

I spent most of the rehearsal handing out envelopes. Each dancer gets one comp, but when I open my envelope, I see that Lynette gave me *three* free tickets—compensation for putting my photo on the poster without asking, I assume. Since Mom already bought her tickets, I can get both Clarissa and Sonya in for free. That leaves one comp unclaimed.

At home, I find a sticky note in Mom's desk. I write, "Just in case you change your mind," press the note onto the ticket and scribble a name on the envelope. After taking the steps down to the fifth floor, I slip it under 5B's door, and hope Jacy takes the hint.

chapter thirty-one

A whirlwind of activity fills the girls' dressing room, which is actually a third-grade classroom. Opening night.

Costumes in rainbow colors hang on movable clothing racks. A portable, full-length mirror leans against the wall. Smaller mirrors are scattered across desks so dancers can do their makeup. Everyone chatters a mile a minute.

Except me. I wish I could Zen out but it's hard to find a quiet place. I'm not the only one. I nod to Samantha, who has also moved into the corner. She and I take a similar approach to our bad behavior: mutual amnesia.

Tonight, she's so nervous she's actually nice. "I really like your solo costume, Ali."

It isn't the costume I'm wearing now, however. The first outfit is a leotard and short, green dance skirt that Quentin wanted the girls in the ensemble to wear.

I know my line. "Thanks. You look beautiful in yours."

Samantha wears a long blue chiffon skirt, several shades lighter than the giant eye. "You don't think the skirt makes me look fat?"

That'll be the day.

Before I come out with the required response—*Of course you don't look fat*—Lynette jogs over.

"Looks like Ali's got an admirer!" She hands me a bouquet of buttery sunflowers. "Five minutes to curtain, everyone!"

Screeches from the little kids.

Sam leans over. "Are the flowers from your mom?"

The card, computer printed by the florist, is tucked inside a small envelope. The first sentence makes me smile. Leave it to Jacy to understand just how nervous I'd be.

Seize the moment, Alicia. You've worked really hard.

See you after the show.

Your best friend

"Not my mom." I drop the note into my messenger bag. "She has to work tonight. She bought tickets for tomorrow."

When it's clear that's all I'm going to say, Samantha humphs toward the other end of the room. Keisha stops brushing green eye shadow.

"They're pretty, Ali." She lowers her voice. "Come on, who sent them? *Shyboy?*"

"My friend Jacy. He lives in my building."

"Wish I had a friend like that." She sighs.

Lynette sticks her head in the doorway. "Places for Fairy Tale Dance! Ali, can you help?"

I stand in the hallway and herd little girls. All wear pastel-colored princess dresses with satin tops and puffy skirts. All really excited—except for one. She has the mournful eyes of someone who thinks she might puke. Even though I can definitely relate, I play big sister.

"You'll do fine, Janella. Once the music starts, it'll be a breeze."

"Promise, Ali?"

I cross my heart. "Don't forget to smile."

"Okay…"

There isn't much else to do but stay limber until Lynette calls for Quentin's piece.

When she does, we quietly take our marks onstage and wait for our cue. After worrying about my solo for so long, dancing in the ensemble is a snap. I feel myself relax as the group moves, completely in sync. We keep the spacing that Quentin drilled into us, and the off-kilter patterns he dreamed up work like a charm. His artistry flows through every one of us, energizing the ensemble the way really good choreography can. Samantha and Blake are right on, too. We are all awarded a huge round of applause at the dance's end.

"This is so fun!" Keisha whispers. "Glad we have two more performances!"

Back in the dressing room, I change into my black costume after the jazz dancers leave. There are so many of them, the noise in the room drops at least a hundred decibels.

Jacqui, who choreographed the trio that's programmed ahead of my solo, stretches on the floor. "How's the house?"

"Real good. I'm sure Lynette's thrilled."

A knock on the door.

"Choreographer's Showcase," Lynette calls. "Break a leg, ladies."

After checking the mirror one last time to make sure no stray hair escaped my bun, I follow Jacqui out of the dressing room. From a darkened wing, I peek into the audience.

The place is packed. Programs rustle. People speak in

hushed voices while they wait for the houselights to dim again. Someone laughs. Video cameras are everywhere.

The small balcony above the main audience area is filled with dancers who've already performed. Lynette has a rule: no one is allowed back in the dressing room, lest they change into street clothes before the entire show is over. Otherwise, parents leave after their kid performs, and the dancers at the end present to a mostly empty house.

Jacqui's trio creates her opening tableau. As soon as the music begins and the stage lights up, people in the house stop shifting.

I scan the audience. White-haired grandparents, bored brothers, proud parents. A man seated audience right catches my attention. I've seen him before but can't place him. Jacqui's dad? Sam's uncle? I stop trying to figure it out, however, as I catch sight of Jacy in an aisle seat.

Something pink is in his lap, but my focus slides to Clarissa and Sonya seated next to him. Yes! The three managed to hook up in the lobby and find seats together.

Now I'm really nervous. I move to the edge of the wings and stand beside the sandbags, ropes and levers that control the fly space. I try to mark my piece, but grow panicked when I can't remember the count. Is it three spins after the contraction—or four?

You're listening to someone else's music. It'll be fine once the Clash comes on.

I plié a bunch of times and wait for the applause that signals the trio's end.

The curtain-call lights come on and the trio bows. The stage dims once more, which is the cue for me to head for the first glow-in-the-dark tape that marks my opening position.

"Break a leg," Jacqui whispers, as we pass each other in the dark.

Deep breath. Music pulses through the speakers. All across the stage, tight areas of light appear, streetlamps in a midnight city. I begin the opening section by moving in and out of darkness: now you see me, now you don't. Each time I hit a light, I strike a different pose. Hand across tilted cheek. Fist into stomach. Arms clasped overhead.

The chains on my costume catch the light. Beams flash into the audience. After two high battements, I glide into the arabesque—*hold, hold*—ready for the tempo change—when it feels like I've been hit by one of the sandbags in the wings.

Pink! Jacy has *roses* in his lap. So who sent the sunflowers to the dressing room?

Not Clarissa and Sonya.

The note told me that.

Not Friends, plural, but Friend. Singular.

My standing leg wavers.

Every synapse in my body screams *Run,* although my muscles, conditioned by years of dance training, whisper *Keep going.*

The tempo changes. I'm supposed to start the Martha Graham contraction that propels me across the stage, but I can't move.

He's here. Sitting in the audience. Watching from behind a camera lens…

Lynette's whisper hisses across the stage. "Ali! Catch up to the count!"

A nightmare come true. After the initial paralysis, adrenaline kicks in. I can't move fast enough. I dart off the stage. The shocked faces of Jacqui and her two dancers, huddled in the wings, are a blur. I barrel past Glen and his duet partner.

Down the hallway into the dressing room. Lock the door behind me, glance at the desk where I put the sunflowers. The bouquet isn't there.

Who took it?

I catch a glimpse of yellow. The flowers are beside my coat, neatly folded on a desk at the far end of the room. Only I'd swear I hung the coat on one of the costume racks.

Did someone go through my things while I watched Jacqui's trio? What if that person *didn't* go back to the audience to see me dance? Is he in here? Hiding in the closet? Standing behind one of the clothes racks, ready to make his move any second…

I stick bare feet into my shoes, grab my coat and get out of Trinity the fastest way I can. The door at the end of the hall.

A screeching alarm sounds. Too late, I notice the sign that says Emergency Exit.

I sprint down Montague, sliding in the dusting of snow that covers the sidewalk. Does the alarm mean everyone in the building will evacuate? Which would include the *guy*.

See you after the show.

Like a hunted deer, I search for a way to blend in. Starbucks!

Steam coats the windows. Once inside, I won't be able to see out but it also means no one can see in. My right leg jiggles uncontrollably as I wait in line. Cappuccino is out of the question, so I order cocoa. I check the door to make sure no one followed. A tap on the counter startles me. The bored barista blows strands of hair from her forehead.

"Name? I need to write it on the cup."

"Sorry. Al—Bob."

"Clever." She looks as if it's anything but. "Don't tell me I gotta serve the Forty Thieves, too."

"Excuse me?"

"Alibaba. That's the name you gave, right?"

"Just Bob."

"Okay, Just Bob." She rings the cash register. "Two ninety-five."

Oh, no! My wallet is in my messenger bag—inside the dressing room. Along with my cell. ChapStick. The keys to the apartment!

"You want the drink or not?"

I shake my head and move away.

See you after the show.

Just as I feared, the stalker knew exactly where I'd be. But staying secret didn't keep him happy for long. Now he wants to talk—or worse—watch me undress in person! Despite the fact that all I have on under the coat is my thin costume, my face feels flushed. He's closing in on me....

I made a huge mistake. I should have stayed with Lynette, explained why I ruined the concert, let her protect me. Instead, I'm alone.

My finger shakes as I wipe a tiny bit of condensation from the window. I'm not sure who I expect to appear in front of the glass. A stranger, standing in the newly fallen snow, holding a sign: I Am Your Stalker.

The circle is so small, however, that I can't see anyone unless they pass directly in front of me. An instant later, they disappear into the steam. Like a magic trick. Now you see 'em, now you don't. Or someone with no peripheral vision.

Jacy!

I let out a moan. When the fire alarm rang, Lynette must have turned on the lights so everyone could see to get out. Is Jacy waiting in front of Trinity with Clarissa and Sonya—

extremely cold, unbelievably pissed off? Then there's Glen and his duet partner. Bet they're furious with me, too.

The window's narrow view seems way too wide.

chapter thirty-two

I have to find Jacy and get my messenger bag with the keys to my apartment. *If* they haven't been stolen.

The street is crowded, the concert definitely over. I keep my head down and retrace my steps. The bleating of a horn gets my attention. I shift my weight, ready to run—

"Ali! It's us." Clarissa sticks her head out of a taxi's front passenger window. The cab pulls to a stop a few feet ahead of me. "We've been looking for you."

"What about Jacy?"

"He's here, too. We got your stuff."

The back door opens. Sonya slides so she's between Jacy and me. My messenger bag lies on the floor. I scramble through it: cell, wallet, keys. Nothing missing.

"Was there smoke?" Sonya asks. "Is that why you ran?"

I can't seem to open my mouth.

Clarissa shakes her head at Sonya. "It's okay. Tell us when we get home." She tells the driver, "425 Clinton."

Jacy, on the far side of the cab, doesn't move. He stares

out of the window as if the secret to the universe is being revealed—or like he's furious at me.

When he finally speaks, he doesn't sound mad. "He was there, Ali, wasn't he?"

My breath catches. "How do you know?"

"Who was where?" Sonya asks.

Neither Jacy nor I say anything.

Clarissa gasps. "Omigod! Did somebody do something to you backstage?"

"No," I whisper. "I just know the creep was at the show."

Sonya turns to Jacy. "How did *you* know?"

Jacy's words float through the cab like a boat adrift in the Hudson River. "Besides the fact that Ali *bolted,* I smelled him."

Sonya's mouth drops open. "What on earth does a perv smell like?"

"Burnt leaves. At least this one does."

The cab stops in front of my building. I fumble for money but Clarissa's already got her wallet out. I look back to make sure no one's come after us. Jacy stands on the sidewalk, disoriented, not sure where to go. The expression on his face says it all—he can't see a thing.

I scoot over, slip my arm through his.

"Follow me," I whisper and guide him into the lobby without either of the girls realizing what's going on.

For once, the elevator is on the ground floor. When we get to my apartment, I turn on every light. Sonya discovers a bottle of brandy at the back of a cabinet. "It's so dusty, Ali, your mom will never miss it."

She brings four glasses and a bag of Doritos in from the kitchen. "Comfort food!"

No one looks the least bit comforted.

Sonya settles on the floor beside the couch. "Okay, Jacy, how exactly did you smell the stalker?"

"I caught a whiff of something as people began to push up the aisle. I'm sure I smelled the same thing in here after Ali got back from Baltimore."

"Could you tell who it was coming from?" Clarissa asks.

Jacy hesitates. "There were too many people. And I was trying to see if Ali would come back onstage. That's why I didn't move when everyone started evacuating."

"Wait!" Sonya cries. "If you smelled the stalker in here, then that means—"

"He broke in to the apartment. When Ali and her mom were away."

My hand tightens on the glass.

"Are you okay?" Clarissa asks.

"I don't know." My tongue feels thick, awkward. "Breaking in to the house? That's pretty extreme. Nothing's missing. Why would someone go through all that trouble and then not take anything?"

Jacy's cheeks grow red. "Maybe he took… I don't know. Personal stuff. Clothing…underwear."

"Eww!" Clarissa shrieks.

I take a sip of brandy to avoid seeing the unasked question on each face.

"I don't know, okay?" I finally say. "It's not like I have Day of the Week panties so I can go, oh, where's Tuesday?"

"Just Hello Kitty," Sonya mutters.

"Sonya!" Clarissa says.

"Sorry." She grabs a handful of chips. "Ali, how did *you* know the guy was there tonight?"

"He sent flowers."

"No way," Clarissa breathes.

"Lynette brought a bouquet into the dressing room just before the show began. There was a note."

"And he signed it? What? Tom the Peeper?" Jacy slaps his glass onto the coffee table. "Stan the Stalker?"

"'Your best friend.' He also wrote, 'See you after the show.'"

Clarissa's hand flies to her mouth. "Did he follow us?" She runs to the window and peeks through the closed venetian blinds. "No one's on the street."

Now you know how creepy it feels.

I cradle the glass. "When I was in the wings, I saw all these people with cameras. It wasn't until I went onstage that I realized *he* sent the flowers and was probably in the audience."

Clarissa turns from the window. "Could it possibly have been Charlie? Maybe he sent them to apologize for being such a turd. Did anyone see him at the concert?"

"Not me," Sonya says.

"Charlie hasn't spoken to me since that day in the library."

"I didn't see him, either," Jacy says a little too casually, which I take to mean *he couldn't see anyone.*

"It could be anybody, actually," I tell them. "Some *dancergirl* freak who found out about the concert. Or Cisco."

"Blue eyes? Works out?" Clarissa asks.

"Yeah."

"Then I saw him."

Too agitated to sit, I pace the room. "That doesn't actually prove he's the stalker. Lynette asked him to tape the performance for the DVD—"

"Hold on!" Clarissa's eyes have grown so big they look like CDs. "Luke Sorezzi was there. I saw him by the bathrooms."

I stop dead. "Are you sure?"

Clarissa nods. "Thought maybe he had a sister in the show."

I shake my head. "I do the class cards. I would have noticed the last name."

"Did he have a camera?" Jacy asks.

Clarissa shrugs helplessly. "I didn't see one. But why else would he go—"

"Because Ali's bookmarked on his computer," Sonya says.

Clarissa stares. "How do you know?"

"I was at his apartment one day. With Laura Hernandez."

I blink. "What were you doing with them?"

Sonya lifts her chin defiantly. "You were all busy. *Dancergirl* this, *dancergirl* that. It's all anyone cared about. Except geniusboy, here, and he already jumped ship. Laura asked if I wanted to hang out after school one day, so I went to Luke's with her. She hates you, you know."

"Me?" I ask. "Because of the videos?"

Sonya shakes her head. "Before that. She thinks it's your fault that Jacy ignores her."

"My fault?" I appeal to him. "I never said anything about Laura! Right?"

"Right." Jacy's hair flops emphatically. "I'll tell her—"

"Don't bother," Sonya says. "I made it perfectly clear that after you moved to private school, you dumped all of us, so she shouldn't take it personally."

"I didn't dump you…" Jacy mutters. "I've been busy."

"Whatever. Then *dancergirl* hit—and that didn't help Laura's attitude. Or Charlie's. Or Josh's for that matter. If I had to hear one more time—" Sonya's hurt is obvious. "Who cares if people thought it was real? It's whatever anyone thinks it is, anyway."

"What's that supposed to mean?" Clarissa asks.

"Laura Hernandez took one look at the party video and

decided, 'Ali's a show-off.' Sorezzi thinks she's a wild girl. Neither's right—and neither's wrong."

"I was *not* showing off. Charlie asked me to do it."

Sonya shakes her head. "This isn't about you, Ali. That's what I'm trying to say. It's about them. It's the internet, for goodness' sake. Once you put it out there, you can't control it. Even if it's innocent. That's the very definition of *viral,* right? Whoever watches is going to think whatever they think for their own reasons."

Somewhere in my brain, a light trips on. "Like Keisha."

"Who?"

"Keisha Watson. At the studio. She's convinced *shyboy*'s younger and that's why he's afraid to talk to me. But Keisha's only fourteen, and really shy herself, so maybe that's the reason she came up with that."

"Exactly!" Sonya looks at us looking at her. "Right now you're all staring at me like you're shocked. Because I'm not as 'smart' as Jacy, or as 'arty' as Ali, or as 'cool-looking' as Clarissa. You think I don't know anything—"

"That's not true," I say loyally.

Sonya waves it aside. "I'm not mad. I'm just saying. People look at me and think, 'boring fat chick.' They do, I know. But they don't realize I read philosophy books and other hard stuff. Even your best friends might not know your deepest secrets."

Jacy stares at the floor like he wishes it would open up so he could disappear into his living room. I think about Sorezzi and his mom. But Sonya's on a roll and doesn't notice.

"That's why you're so upset, Ali. I mean, of course, it's totally evil that there's a stalker or Peeping Tom or whatever, but it's worse because of what went out online. The videos Charlie shot were fine because you wanted to do them. They looked like you and danced like you, but it was never really Alicia Ruffino. It was a made-up character. But the stuff in your bedroom *was* you—your private self that you never agreed to show anyone."

Clarissa sits up straight. "Does this mean Laura Hernandez shot the bedroom video? Because she hates Ali?"

Sonya shrugs. "Seems like way too much effort for her."

"But according to your theory," Jacy says, "that slacker attitude could be her public face. So we can't count her out."

"Or Sorezzi," Clarissa says. "The smell might be some hopped-up weed he's smoking—"

I shake my head. "I'm pretty sure it's not Luke—"

Clarissa's cell interrupts. Two seconds later, Sonya's beeps, too. Clarissa's face turns ashen.

"What's wrong?" Jacy asks.

Without a word, she holds out her phone. A video plays on the screen. Bright lights on a stage so there's no mistaking who's frozen in arabesque. To my everlasting shame, I watch myself flee into the wings like a frightened rabbit.

chapter thirty-three

"The atom is almost all empty space. If the nucleus of a plutonium atom were a grapefruit sitting in front of you, the electrons orbiting around it would be like ninety-four grains of sand revolving around the entire borough of Brooklyn."

Out of everything Mr. Kuperman talked about in physics, that's the only thing I understand. As I lie on the pullout couch the morning after the concert, his gravelly voice fills my head.

"Sometimes an electron jumps to another orbit. Scientists call that a quantum leap. When an electron makes that leap, it either takes in or gives up energy, but it never stays the same."

That's me. An electron that disappears from one orbit only to reappear in another. In this new one, I lose energy. I feel the emptiness of the universe as I've never felt it before.

My worst nightmares. Plural. The pervert's definitely stalking me. And I made an absolute, total fool of myself. Not only onstage but, with the wonder of the internet, for the entire world to see, forever.

I'm not sure how long I lay without moving. Mom's asleep,

having come home to a somewhat disheveled pajama party. Only no one had on pajamas. It wasn't just Jacy and me that she found passed out in the living room. Clarissa and Sonya stayed, too. Like campers huddled around a fire to keep the bears away, nobody wanted to sleep in my room. After we put away the brandy bottle and washed the glasses, Sonya and I unfolded the pullout. Clarissa, Sonya and I squashed in together. Jacy laid out a sleeping bag half-under the coffee table.

The phone rings. Jacy grabs the receiver before it can awaken Mom. I struggle up.

"Lynette," he mouths.

"I'm not taking it," I whisper.

Clarissa stirs. "You should talk to her, Ali. Explain."

Jacy brings the phone into the kitchen. I go to the bathroom to pee and brush my teeth. When I return, both Clarissa and Sonya are wide-awake.

"What's going on?"

"Lynette wants you to do the show tonight," Jacy says. "She'll cut the solo but says it's important for you to remain in Quentin's piece. She said you danced beautifully—"

My hand goes up to stop him. "No way!"

Clarissa looks seriously worried. "It's like falling off a horse. If you don't get onstage tonight, you might never go back."

"Fine with me. I am never dancing again."

"Ali!" Clarissa breathes. "You don't really mean that—"

Jacy gives me a look that says, *I understand.* "Let her be, Clarissa. I'll call Lynette back. Tell her Ali can't do it."

I return to the couch, crawl under the blanket and huddle against my pillow. A short while later, a finger gently pokes the quilt.

"I asked about the flowers," Jacy says.

Something in his tone makes me sit up.

"Lynette said the regular deliveryman from Carson's brought them, so I called the store. The person who answered remembered the order because it was strange."

Sonya and Clarissa settle beside me in a vain attempt at protection.

"Yesterday afternoon, the lady was alone in the shop. She went into the storeroom for just a minute. By the time she got back, an envelope was on the counter. Inside were specific directions on where to bring the bouquet, instructions for the card and cash. She didn't see who put it there."

Clarissa shivers. "The guy's definitely sneaky."

"I also asked Lynette to email me the reservation sheet. I made up some excuse about how we need to call your friends who reserved tickets. She said she had it on her computer." He stands. "Let me see if she sent it."

Nobody says anything. We hear the printer's ratchety noise. When Jacy returns to the living room, he doesn't look happy.

"There are a lot of names."

"We sold out," I remind him. "Plus, how do we know the stalker used his real name to reserve a seat? He could have lied."

Sonya looks startled. "I never thought of that!"

Jacy shakes his head. "The person would use his—or her—real name if they live around here. If someone at the box office recognized them, using a fake name would be suspicious."

"But what if it's some *dancergirl* creep?" I ask.

"Even if it is, the creepoid lives in the neighborhood. The flowers are the key. Think about it. Dropping off an envelope at the exact moment the florist goes into the back room means someone watched the place because they didn't want to be recognized." Jacy holds up a hand. "It's not a hundred percent, but I bet it's someone who lives around here."

"Okay, but at least we can rule out people at school. You know, Charlie, Sorezzi."

Clarissa looks up at me. "How come?"

"Because of what Charlie said when Jacy and I met him at the Promenade. The first stalker video was uploaded during a football game. The big one between WiHi and Marshall. Charlie insisted he couldn't have done it because he was at the game. And you know Sorezzi was there, selling weed under the bleachers like always."

Sonya sits up. "Ali, do you remember exactly what time the video hit the net?"

"Why?"

She runs her hand through her coal-black hair. "Just tell me."

"8:25. Something like that, right, Jace?"

A perplexed look crosses his face as he nods. Whatever Sonya's going for, she's ahead of both Jacy and me.

"Charlie could have done it," she announces.

"But he was at the game—"

"That's what he *said*," Jacy interrupts. "But, really, Ali, do we have proof?"

"Well, yeah," Clarissa says. "I saw him. We both saw him, right, Sonya? Charlie sat a couple of rows in front of us."

Sonya nods emphatically. "I remember what he was wearing. A navy-blue coat and that Harry Potter scarf."

"What the heck's a Harry Potter scarf?" Jacy snorts. "Low-rent Invisibility Cloak? Only your neck disappears."

Sonya waves her hand impatiently. "It's maroon and gold, which are Gryffindor colors in the books. They're also USC colors. You know, USC film school, the school he never stops talking about—"

"I've seen the scarf," I say. "But what does that have to do with Charlie being at the game or not?"

Sonya's eyes move rapidly, like she's watching a movie. "He was there at kickoff, which was at 7:00. Remember, Clarissa, I brought my dad's camera. He's into electronics and had just gotten a new lens. Telephoto. I wanted to try it out. He said, sure, just don't break it or lose it."

Somewhere outside, a horn honks. Inside the living room, no one moves.

"It's not even fifteen minutes later," Sonya continues. "I'm fooling around with the lens, using it like a telescope, watching the other side of the bleachers. I move it over the field, taking a picture whenever something looks interesting. Then I swing it toward the end zone. I want to check how far I can see with it. That's when I notice the scarf." She looks at me. "It was weird, because Charlie was just sitting two rows below us. So I look down, and sure enough, there's an empty spot."

Clarissa's confused, too. "He could have been buying a hot dog from the senior-class stand."

Sonya shakes her head. "No, he was on the other side. By the exit. Charlie was definitely on his way out, talking to someone really tall."

My heart pounds. "Who?"

"I don't know. The guy's back was to me but I know it was Charlie talking to him because of the scarf."

"It's possible that someone else at the game had a USC scarf," Jacy says. "Doesn't quite prove that Charlie lied."

"It does if I still have the photo."

Jacy pounces. "Do you?"

"I think so. When I got home that night, I downloaded everything I shot to my computer before giving the camera back to Dad. I'm pretty sure I didn't delete it." She holds up a hand. "I know what you're going to ask. I waited for Charlie to come back to the bleachers because I wanted to take another shot. A close-up. I thought I could play around in Photoshop and do something cool with the two pictures. But I didn't see him the rest of the night."

Jacy glances at me. "So now there are two questions of the day. Why did Charlie lie to us?"

"And who was that other guy?"

chapter thirty-four

We decide to meet at Sonya's in an hour. Clarissa's priority is getting home so she can change out of the clothes she slept in. For the rest of us, it's not a new outfit but a hot shower that's high on the list of life necessities.

Last night's snowfall didn't leave much on the streets. With the clouds gone from the sky, however, the weather is frigid. I pull on a thermal before sticking my head through a ribbed-neck sweater. Jacket, hat, scarf—I'm as warm as I can be.

I text Jacy: Ready?

His reply is brief: Meet you there.

I'm anxious to see if Sonya found the photo so I text back: don't b long.

Halfway out the door, I remember Mom. She's fast asleep so I prop a note against the sugar bowl: "Went to Sonya's. See you soon."

The air is so cold it hurts to breathe. But it also means that everyone I see hurries, too. No one lingers, no one's watching me. At least not on the street.

Sonya lives on the other side of Montague so I take my

usual path through the Heights. I'm thinking about the person Charlie was with—*tall and thin*—when I practically bump into someone.

No way! It's Lynette, hurrying toward the studio. "Ali! Are you coming to see me? Did you change your mind?"

"No. I'm not doing the show."

"Alicia, please talk to me. You at least owe me an explanation."

I sigh. "For a minute. I'm supposed to be someplace."

The studio is dark and cold. The dancers have been at Trinity all week, so Lynette turned the heat off. She flips on the lights and fiddles with the space heater beside the counter. It'll be at least half an hour before the place warms up, not that I plan to be here that long.

Lynette pulls off her gloves, although she leaves her coat on. I don't mess with a single article of clothing. She sits on one of the two tall counter chairs. On the wall behind her, a Winter Fest poster stares down at us.

"Ali, what happened last night?" Lynette asks gently.

I ignore her question to ask one of my own. "Did you make Eva include my solo in Choreographer's Showcase?"

She blinks. "Excuse me?"

"The solo. Eva had three spots to give out. The dance wasn't even finished when she chose it. There were other pieces she could have picked. Finished ones. Better ones—"

Lynette eyes me curiously. "Just because the solo needed work doesn't mean Eva didn't see the potential. That's how choreography works. It gets better as you rehearse and make changes."

I don't have to look at the poster to see myself. "Why don't I believe you?"

She picks up a pencil thoughtfully. "Is that what happened?

In the middle of the performance you decided you didn't *deserve* it? That doesn't make sense. Unless someone said something just before you went on. Told you that you only got the solo because I insisted." I refuse to look at her. "Who was it, Ali?"

I shake my head, even as my cheeks burn. I refuse to finger Samantha because it's not as if I hadn't played the same evil game.

"Fine," Lynette murmurs. "I bet I know who it was."

"That's not even the point."

"Then what is?" When I don't respond, she taps the counter. "I don't understand. You're a serious dancer, Ali. You've been in lots of shows so it couldn't have been a terrible case of stage fright. I know you want a career. I think you're good enough or I wouldn't have encouraged you. But you've got to understand that this is part of a career. Backbiting, jealousy, auditioning for things and not getting them *not* because you aren't good enough—but because you don't have the look the choreographer wants. Or getting something because of your look." She shakes her head. "If it's too hard to deal with, you're probably right. You really should consider doing something else with your life."

"I can deal with that part. I mean, I think I can. It's the stalking part that makes me want to puke—"

Lynette gives me a sharp glance. "What stalking part? Is someone— Oh, Lord! Is that why you were so upset about the posters? Somebody's *stalking you?*"

All I can do is nod.

"Do you know who it is?"

I shake my head.

"When did it start? Have you actually seen the person?" Her hand hits the counter. "Did someone touch you—"

"No. And it could just be a Peeping Tom. A Peeping Tom doesn't...touch anyone."

"Beside the point. Did you go to the police?"

It's too much to get into the fine details of whether or not Mr. Ryan is actually a cop at the moment, so I just nod.

"That was the problem last night," I say. "The stalker was in the audience. Watching—"

Lynette sinks back into the chair. "Oh, Ali, I am so sorry." She bites her lip as she tries to process what I'm telling her. "How did you know the guy was there if you don't know who he is?"

"The flowers you brought into the dressing room. And there was other stuff."

A piece of the puzzle falls into place for her. "So that's why your friend asked about the delivery. I wondered about it after I hung up. Then I figured you wanted to thank whoever sent them—and for some reason you needed the reservation list to figure it out. Are you sure it isn't someone you know? I thought I read somewhere that stalkers go after people known to them."

I fiddle with the ends of my scarf. "Not always. It could be a stranger who saw *dancergirl* online."

She lowers her eyes guiltily. "I had no idea."

That's when I decide that maybe she knows something that might help. I pull a chair next to hers. "But you're right, too, Lynette. It could be someone I know. Someone *you* know."

Lynette grows still. "Who?"

I watch her closely. "Cisco."

She recoils as if bitten by a poisonous snake. "That's absurd."

"Why? He hangs around here an awful lot. He designed

the poster and picked my picture to put on it. He came to rehearsals and was at the performance last night."

"He's doing me a favor. I'm the one who asked him to tape the show so I can sell DVDs. Cisco has no reason to stalk anyone. He's got plenty of women—" She stops herself, blushes and reaches for the phone. "You have to decide right now. If you're not going to dance tonight, I need to call Quentin so he can re-block the ensemble without you…"

I press the hang-up button on the phone console. "Are you creeping around with Cisco, Lynette?"

She bristles. "Ali—"

"You are, aren't you?"

"Of course not."

"Did you even hear what you said? 'He's got plenty of women.' Not 'He's got Eva.'" I back away as if that poisonous snake just reared its ugly head at me. "Blake heard him and Eva fighting about someone in the alley behind Moving Arts. Does Eva know it's you?" I stare down the hallway and let out a breath. "That explains it. Cisco came in to find *you* audition night. Not me. Or her. But I was here, so he lied—"

"What are you talking about?"

I point down the hall. "Cisco came in the back door when I was holding down the fort before auditions began. He saw the lights on in Studio A and thought you were here. The back door had been left unlocked. And here I went and spent weeks worrying he was after me all because of that night—"

"Ali—"

"Don't make excuses, Lynette. I don't want to know what you all are doing." With a quick pivot, I head for the front door. "I have way too much sleaze in my own life, thank you very much."

★ ★ ★

By the time I get to Sonya's, Jacy is beside himself. Worried more than Mom would be.

"Where were you?" he barks. "Don't you pick up your cell? I called at least three times—"

"I'm sorry. I ran into Lynette and went to talk to her in the studio. I didn't hear anything. My phone's on vibrate because of the show last night—"

"It's okay, Ali," Clarissa soothes. "We just thought—"

"I'm so sorry. I can imagine what you thought. But you won't believe what I found out."

I give them the highlights of the Lynette conversation.

"Gross!" Sonya shudders. "Isn't she a lot older than Cisco?"

"Yeah, but that isn't any of my concern. The good news is we can pretty much knock Cisco off the list of possible stalkers because he wasn't at the studio to see me." I turn to Sonya. "Did you find the photo you took at the game?"

"Yep. It's exactly the way I remembered." She holds up the copy she printed. "It's not the best color quality but you can see that Charlie's talking to the guy while he exits."

A quick glance confirms she's right. I can't, however, tell who he's leaving with.

I stand. "Well, which of us is calling Sennñor Liu?"

Charlie looks totally confused when the four of us pile into his bedroom. "What the—what are you guys doing here? I thought only Clarissa was coming over."

Sonya nudges me and then glances meaningfully at the walls. Charlie's room is covered in movie posters. Mostly horror flicks.

Quietly, Jacy closes the door. Charlie glances at him suspiciously. "Okay, if this was *The Godfather* you'd be showing me the severed head right now. Or asking me to go for a little ride. But since none of you can drive—"

"Quit clowning," I say. "Show him the photo, Sonya."

Charlie opens his mouth to sass me back. Nothing except a squeak comes out, however, because Sonya has shoved the photo under his face.

He swallows. "What's going on?"

"I think you should tell us," Jacy says. "We're especially interested in why you lied to me and Ali."

"First, I don't know what you're talking about. Second, where did this photo come from?"

"My dad's camera." Charlie looks mystified so Sonya adds, "He didn't take it. I did. At the football game. But you asked—"

"I know what I asked. Do you have any more photos of me?" Sonya shakes her head. Charlie lets out a breath. "So why are you here? You took a picture three months ago and show up now, all pissed off for some reason. I don't get it."

"This was taken the night that *Hot Diggity* video was uploaded to Zube," I explain. "The next morning, Jace and I met you at the Promenade. You insisted you couldn't have been the one who did it because you were at the game. Except you weren't."

Charlie gives me a "you're crazy" look. "Except I was. This proves it."

"What this proves is that you left the game. Right after kickoff. And you never came back." Sonya holds up a hand. "Don't try to deny it, Charlie. 'Rissa and I sat a few rows above you. I'm positive that you never went back to your seat. The very next day you lied about it to Ali and Jace."

Charlie waves at the photo. "So somehow this is supposed

to prove I made the stalker video? I told them then—and I'll tell you now. I didn't. I swear."

"Who's in the photo with you?" Jacy counters. "Maybe he did it."

"How should I know who it is?"

"Because you're talking to him," Sonya says.

"Maybe I bumped into him so I'm apologizing. What does it even matter?"

"It matters because you could have shot the video Wednesday night," Jacy says smugly, "edited it and slipped it to this guy to upload on Friday."

Charlie laughs. "And people think I see too many movies. Who am I supposed to be, some kind of superspy?"

Clarissa has been uncharacteristically quiet. Now, she sits next to Charlie and points to the mysterious skinny dude. "I don't think you're a spy. But why don't you want to tell us who this is? If you didn't go home to upload the video like you said, then he can be your, um, whatchacall it?"

"Alibi," Sonya says.

Charlie pounds his fist against the bed frame. "How many times do I have to say this? He can't be my alibi because *I don't know him*."

Despite his adamant protest, something doesn't ring true. Before I can figure out what it is, Charlie folds his arms. "Anyway, I don't need an alibi because I can prove I didn't shoot that video." He points to his computer. "Check my hard drive. All the footage I have of Ali is footage she knows I shot."

"You could have deleted it," I tell him. "After uploading."

He shakes his head. "No director deletes footage. You never know when you're going to need something you shot."

"Sounds like a load of bull to me," Jacy says.

"Believe what you want, Strode, but I am not Ali's stalker. Which means you all are wasting your time." He opens his bedroom door. "Get out!"

The small table is littered with torn packets of sugar, drippy wooden stir sticks—and four lattes. After leaving Charlie's apartment, Sonya, Jacy, Clarissa and I needed caffeine in the worst way. Not one of us got much sleep.

Clarissa stirs the milky drink. "Something isn't right."

"You think?" Jacy tastes his coffee, adds more sugar. "He's a lying sack of doo-doo."

Sonya does an odd snort-laugh. "What are you? Three years old?"

Jacy motions to the table next to us, where a frazzled mom and her toddler share a cup of hot chocolate. "No, but he is."

"Very considerate," Sonya says. "If only Charles were as considerate and told us the truth."

"Everyone thinks he's lying?" I ask.

Three heads nod.

"And you all think the skinny dude has something to do with this?"

Again, the simultaneous head nod. They could work up an act, take it out on the road.

Over at the next table, the mom and toddler make "get up and go" noises. She bundles up the kid, and he squirms. My gaze returns to my friends.

"Where does that leave us?"

Jacy grimaces. "In the same place. With almost the same questions. What is Charlie hiding? And who is that guy?"

There's nothing more we can do at the moment, so we separate. I let myself back into the apartment as quietly as I can. Mom's still asleep. I'm relieved because I don't want to talk to her. I don't want to talk to anyone.

I throw myself on my bed. But every time I close my eyes, the videotape of me running offstage loops obsessively. Finally, I head over to my computer. Maybe it's not as bad as I think.

I find the video on Zube and hit Play. Instead of the Clash, though, different music plays. A bunch of out-of-tune violin strikes, like something from a Hitchcock movie. Confused, I stare at the screen.

That isn't the tape I saw last night.

My heart skips a beat. It's a remix. Someone downloaded last night's video to their own computer and overlaid different music. I scroll over to the Related Videos list. Other remixes are posted, too.

Shocked, I click the next one. A short guy, wearing a wig and skirt—his hairy legs stick out instead of tights—mimics me. He freezes dramatically, does a fake scream and runs offscreen.

People think it's the funniest thing.

I expect my cell to buzz. Somebody will send a link. The phone, however, stays silent. Clarissa, Jacy and Sonya must have dozed off when they got home so they haven't seen all this crap. Or they did—and are afraid to tell me.

No one that I know calls or texts, which may be the worst sign of all.

Too agitated to stay in my room, I pad into the kitchen for a glass of water. I'm startled to see Mom at the table. "I didn't hear you get up."

She holds a cup of strong, black coffee. "Your door was closed so I thought you were taking a nap before the show tonight. I saw Jacy and the girls when I got home this morning. Figured you had a celebratory party." She pats the chair next to her, smiles. "Come, *mija,* tell me all about it."

Instead of sitting down, I move to the sink. Fill a glass with water. "It didn't go too great. The fire alarm went off in the middle of the show and the audience had to evacuate."

Mom blinks. "Was there an actual fire?"

I shake my head. "Electrical malfunction."

"Ay, pobrecita!" She gives me her patented, sympathetic nurse tsk-tsk. "It'll go better tonight, I'm sure. I can't wait. Miranda from work is coming. And on Sunday, Gerald and Annie—"

I try not to look horrified. It never occurred to me that Mom might bring her friends. "You have to call them. The show's not happening."

"What do you mean?" Mom stops midsip.

"Lynette phoned. Because it's the weekend, she can't get the alarm fixed." The lie rolls off my tongue so smoothly I almost believe it myself. "She can't let anyone in until it's figured out."

"But you all worked so hard!" Mom protests.

"She'll try to reschedule but not till January. All the private-school kids get off this week and a lot of them go away for Christmas."

"That's terrible, *mija.*"

I break off a piece of bread, shred it into pieces. "Doing the show is too stressful, anyway. I don't think I'm cut out to be a dancer."

Mom laughs. "That's just a horrible first performance talking. And maybe a little case of stage fright. You'll get over it—"

"How would you know?" My anger flares like one of those California wildfires. Quick, hot, out of control. "You've never gotten onstage in your life! Lynette told me everyone— Oh, forget it."

I stalk out of the room.

"Ali, wait!" Mom cries. "What did Lynette say?"

I can't explain. Any of it. I'm in so deep, I wouldn't know where to begin.

chapter thirty-five

When I get to school on Monday, hidden deep in my hoodie, it's Dawn Chevananda who's the hot topic instead of me. Whispers circulate all morning. She was whisked to the emergency room Sunday afternoon. If she hadn't gotten there when she did, she might have died.

Laura Hernandez shows up late for American History. She and Dawn have been friends since forever. After a whispered conversation, Mrs. Fegarsky raps her knuckles on the whiteboard.

"Listen up, people. Laura has news."

"I just talked to Dawn's mom," Laura announces. "The doctors have been pumping her with antibiotics since yesterday and her fever's down. They think it's bacterial meningitis but won't know until the test comes back."

A murmur goes around the room.

"Is it catching?" Josh yells.

"I'm not sure," Mrs. Fegarsky says. "Make yourself useful, Josh. Get on the computer in the back and find out."

"Can we make get-well cards?" Elora asks.

Although that's a little second grade-ish, everyone, including Mrs. Fegarsky, is more than ready for vacation.

"Excellent idea, Elora. I'm sure Dawn will appreciate it. I might even have some construction paper in the back closet...."

Mrs. Fegarsky hunts for scissors, colored pencils, markers. The class dissolves into excited chatter. In the middle of the confusion, there's a knock on the door. A familiar voice calls out.

"Mrs. Fegarsky, Ali needs to go to the office."

I look over, surprised. Sonya's not an office monitor. When the teacher nods, I grab my messenger bag and slip out the door. "What's going on?"

She moves quickly down the hall. "I want to show you something. Someone, actually."

We scoot down the steps to the first floor. Sonya takes the left archway and pushes through the double doors that lead into the annex. The tile floors are brighter, the rooms newer. She points to a glass window set into a closed door. "Peek in."

Sonya moves so no one in the room can see her. It's the computer lab. Even before I peer in, I know exactly what I'll find. Rows of computers with headsets. Kids working on projects, Mr. Marcus, tall and thin, leaning over to help someone—

"Is that *him?*" I gasp.

"Yep," Sonya breathes. "Charlie's mystery man."

"How did you figure it out?"

"That's my class. I asked for a bathroom pass so I could get you. See, Logan was on the computer to my right and needed help. Mr. Marcus went over. I was curious, because Logan's, like, the biggest computer freak in the world. When I checked to see what was going on, I was in the same position as Charlie was in the picture. Looking *up* at Mr. Marcus."

My head reels. Computer geek as stalker makes sense. Still...

"This isn't proof, Sonya. A million people are tall and thin."

"But a million people don't have a weird, brownish mole shaped like a whale on the back of their hand." She takes out her cell. "I snapped a picture when Mr. Marcus wasn't looking."

"I still don't get why you think he's the guy."

"I spent most of yesterday afternoon blowing up parts of that photo. It was killing me that we didn't know who Charlie was talking to. When I enlarged the guy's hand, I saw the mole. Same as the one in that room."

"What do we do now? Confront Mr. Marcus?"

Sonya shakes her head. "We should talk to Charlie first."

"Why?"

"Because he lied—and I want to know why. There's no way he didn't know who it was."

Down the hallway, a door opens—and closes. The new French teacher exits his classroom. Immediately, Sonya and I turn to the nearest locker. Teachers are supposed to ask anyone they see in the hall for a pass, but the guy's on his cell. After he walks by, I turn back to Sonya.

"Maybe Charlie really didn't know who it was when he looked at the picture. None of us did."

"But you aren't volunteering in the computer lab."

"And Charlie is?"

Sonya nods. "Yep. He switched his schedule in October. He works second period because no one else signed up and Mr. Marcus needed someone to help."

"Wow." A pair of giggling sophomores walk past us. Sonya

and I don't bother to turn away. "Let's talk to him right after school. Get back inside, Sonya. Mr. Marcus might wonder what's taking so long."

Charlie dumps his backpack onto the cracked leather seat of a back booth at the pizzeria. Clarissa slides next to him, blocking him in. Sonya and I sit across from them. I'd texted Jacy but he's stuck in Manhattan.

Go ahead without me was his response.

So we did.

"You have fifteen minutes," Charlie tells us. "I've got an after-school job at Heights Videology. They wanted someone who knows movies for the holiday rush. The kind of stuff you can't find online."

"That's you," I say.

"Yeah." He eyes me warily. "What's up now? Did you find another photo of me taken, oh, when I was eight?"

I pull off my gloves. "Don't like it, do you? Having someone take pictures of you without asking permission."

"Old news, Ali. I got your permission and you know it." Charlie leans forward. "Are you going to hold this against me for the rest of my life?"

Sonya moves a glass shaker filled with Parmesan cheese out of the way. She pulls the shot of Mystery Man's hand from her backpack and places it next to her cell, set to the photo she took in the computer lab.

"Like you just implied, Charlie, let's not go round and round." She points to her cell. "That's Mr. Marcus's hand. I took it in the computer lab today. The photo you see before you was blown up from the shot I took at the football field. We know you know him. Here's your chance to clear things up. Before Ali goes to the police—"

Charlie straightens. "Whoa—you can't do that. He didn't do anything wrong. And he's not the stalker, if that's why you're here."

"How do you know?"

Charlie looks like he'll be sick. "If I tell you something, you cannot tell anyone else."

The three of us exchange looks. Sonya nods. "You've got our word as long as it has nothing to do with Ali."

"It doesn't." Charlie plays with the pepper mill. "You guys are right. I lied. I went to the football game with the sole purpose of—" he makes quotes with his fingers "—*running into him.*"

"Mr. Marcus?" Clarissa asks.

"His name is Leo. In case anybody saw us, we planned to say that we went to the game separately, got bored and happened to leave at the same time. We got to talking about computers...."

"Why didn't you tell us this in the first place?" Sonya demands.

Charlie hesitates.

"Because *that's* the lie," Clarissa says. "They didn't just talk about computers. It was a date."

"With a teacher?" I gasp.

"He's not. He's a teacher's assistant. WiHi can't afford a real computer teacher so they hire him for four hours a day. He goes to Queens College at night." He looks at me, pleading. "He's not even an adult. He's nineteen. That's only three years older than me."

Sonya leans back in the booth. "And you're worried he could lose his job if someone in the office finds out, right?"

Charlie nods. An awkward silence falls over the table. Talk about secrets. A whole lot of information just got dropped into our laps, although none of it has anything to do with the stalker.

It's not as if the news comes as a total shock. Clarissa, Sonya and I have wondered if Charlie was gay ever since tenth grade. But not even Clarissa had the guts to ask—and Charlie wasn't exactly blasting the news around school.

"You should have trusted us when we first came to you," she tells him gently. "We wouldn't have said anything. Ali's been worried sick trying to figure out who the peeper is. We've all been worried sick."

"I'm sorry. It's just—I was shocked when you showed up with the picture. We thought no one had seen us." He looks down. "It was my first real date."

Clarissa gives him a motherly pat on his shoulder. "Did you have a good time?"

He nods shyly.

"Cool!" She grins, delighted that one truth, at least, is finally out in the open. "You know, Charles, I've been waiting for this moment ever since we got to high school!"

"So have I." Charlie returns the grin, then looks at me. "I'm sorry I was such a jerk about *dancergirl*. If you want me to help find the creep, I'm down."

"I have no idea who it is. Or what you could do."

"Think about it," he says. "I will, too."

When I let myself into the apartment, Mom is putting on makeup. She wears a red satin shirt and short black skirt.

"You look pretty," I tell her. "What's the occasion?"

"X-ray's having a holiday party. Thought I'd stop in before my shift. Oh, before I forget. You got a package. I put it in your room."

"Who's it from?"

"I'm not sure." She leans into the mirror to finish brushing mascara. "Did you buy a Christmas present for someone that had to be shipped?"

I shake my head although Mom doesn't notice. She's busy choosing a lipstick. With a jolt, I realize I haven't even started Christmas shopping. Someone could have bought something for *me*. Jacy? Clarissa? She finds stuff online all the time.

The box is white, the kind you get at every post office in the country. My name, address and apartment number are on the front—although there's no return address. The box rattles a bit when I shake it. I know I should wait for Christmas morning but curiosity gets the better of me.

Using the sharp end of a pair of scissors, I slit the tape. Inside the box is a bed of pink tissue paper. A ballerina doll with Barbie-style tits stares up at me. A printed note sticks out from under the tutu.

Just a suggestion.

With an equal mixture of horror and disgust, I stare at the doll's privates. She's wearing thong underwear.

Mom walks in. Instinctively, I pull the tutu down.

She glances at the box. "Cute. From Baltimore?"

"I'm not sure."

"No card?"

I shake my head. "Not even a return address."

"That's strange." She shrugs. "Maybe Teresa forgot to put in a card. Or she ordered it online and it didn't come with one." She wags a finger at me and smiles playfully. "You probably should have waited to open it."

If I had, Mom would have gotten the shock of her life. I close my eyes at the thought of *that* scene.

"Something wrong, Ali? You look…upset." Mom settles beside me. "Having those shows canceled on you is rough, isn't it? Listen, *mija,* I don't have to go to the party. I can eat dinner here. We haven't spent much time together lately—"

"No!" The last thing I need is to feel guilty about messing up her life. "Go to the party, Mom. Really, I'm okay."

She puts her arm around me. "You sure? I don't mind."

"I'd much rather think of you having fun than sitting with me all night."

She gives me a squeeze. "You're a treasure. Don't let anyone ever tell you different. We'll have a good time on Christmas, I promise."

"Go on, you'll be late."

We air-kiss so as not to mess up her lipstick. With a sharp click of her heels, she's gone.

Jacy's furious. I half expect him to heave the doll through my window. "What kind of idiot sends something like this?"

"The kind that's stalking me. We've got to be realistic, Jace. This guy is definitely not a Peeping Tom. Maybe he started that way, but now he's doing more and more pervy stuff. Showing up at Winter Fest, sending this…horrid thing. I can't take it anymore."

Jacy kicks the box the doll came in.

"Point being," I continue, "we can't keep playing detective. We're not getting anywhere and we could screw things up royally for someone else. Can you imagine if we'd actually accused Mr. Marcus? Then everyone finds out he's hooked up with a student. We would have ruined his life."

"It's not your fault. Charlie shouldn't have kept it secret."

"Oh, right. Like you're not keeping anything from your

friends. I sort of think that you, of all people, would understand why Charlie didn't tell."

Jacy is quiet.

"I'm scared, Jace. We have to go to the cops. Even if Mom
finds out. I don't care if I'm grounded. I'm afraid to go anywhere."

"That's a lie," Jacy mumbles bitterly.

"What's that supposed to mean?"

"You were at Rockefeller Plaza the other night. Luke
Sorezzi stood right beside you. I don't think that was coincidence."

Apparently, I can't keep any part of my life private. "You
saw the photo on the fan site?"

Jacy shrugs. "I've been checking the internet."

"Did you see those horrible remixes?"

"Yes. But I was hoping you hadn't."

"Well, I did. And don't think I'm keeping much from you.
The night with Luke was a disaster. Which I do *not* need to
be reminded about."

"Okay, then." Jacy cheers up—until his gaze falls on the
doll. "Let's go talk to Mr. Ryan one last time. See if he has
any ideas. If not, we go to the cops."

chapter thirty-six

Mr. Ryan stands in the open doorway of his brownstone. "It's too windy to talk out here and my apartment's a mess. Head on over to the deli. I'll get my jacket and follow."

It takes less than three minutes to get to the restaurant. Jacy and I head for a corner booth. A table full of guys eating burgers nudge each other.

"Been looking for more video, gorgeous," one of them says. "Something a little more fun than running off a stage."

"How about lap dancing?" another hoots.

Jacy stops dead.

"Ignore them," I beg. "Please! I don't want a scene."

I tug Jacy into the corner. Before he slides into the booth, he lifts his middle finger. Childish, but I appreciate the thought.

Mr. Ryan shows up. Doris, the deli's longtime waitress, follows close behind. She carries plastic-covered menus, has a green pad in her apron pocket and a stubby pencil tucked behind an ear. After we order, Jacy tells Mr. Ryan about the Stalker's latest activities—the concert freak-out video, the doll.

"Ali and I think he's upping things. If he was only watching before, he might have crossed to the stalking side."

"You do know I've talked to my copper pals, right? I asked them to keep it under wraps, not visit you and your mom so as not to worry either of you unnecessarily. The situation is being monitored."

"Thanks. I appreciate it." I lean forward. "But like Jacy said, it feels like in the last week, he's getting, well, bolder."

Before Mr. Ryan can respond, Doris returns.

"Here you are, folks." Deftly, the waitress slides three plates of apple pie onto the speckled Formica tabletop and sets out the drinks: cocoa for me, Coke for Jacy, coffee for Mr. Ryan.

"You want anything else, Tommy, just holler," she says.

Mr. Ryan pours cream into his coffee, stirs thoughtfully. "Okay, I can see you're upset. Let's start with the easy stuff. What about someone from school? Has there been anything in your locker? Notes inside an English book?"

"Nothing like that." I look at Jacy. "We actually ruled out a couple of people at WiHi. Like Charlie, the guy who uploaded the original footage."

Jacy nods. "We thought maybe he was mad because Ali wouldn't shoot any more videos for him."

"Sounds smart. You're absolutely sure he didn't do it?"

"He has an airtight alibi," Jacy says.

"Somebody's watched a lot of TV," Ryan notes drily. "Okay. I agree that it's probably not a school chum. He'd have easy access at Irving and would have left something there. So that means it's either a stranger—or someone else who knows you."

"Like who?" I ask.

Mr. Ryan chews a bit of pie. "Someone who's been inside

your apartment. See, it's the doll that interests me. Why did he send that specific thing?"

I glance at Jacy. "I have a collection. Dolls from around the world."

"Ahh! Okay. Okay. Who would know that? Who's been in your room? Electrician? Uncle? An old boyfriend of your mom's—"

"Hold on. The last guy my mom dated was in the apartment recently. Not my room. At least not that I know of."

"Tell me about him," Mr. Ryan says.

I go into the whole Andrew story. How Mom dumped him, the way he snuck in to get his jacket.

"He had keys?" Mr. Ryan asks.

I nod. "About six months after they started going out, Mom thought he should have a set in case there was an emergency. I told her I'd be okay if something happened when she wasn't home, but she insisted. I guess she forgot to get them back."

"Or he purposefully didn't return them," Jacy says.

"I made sure to get them before he left the apartment this time," I say.

"Could he have decided to stalk Ali to get back at her mom?" Jacy asks.

"Wouldn't be the first time. Not by a long shot." Mr. Ryan pushes his plate away, pops a mint. "Okay, Alicia, here comes the hard question. When he was dating your mother did he ever do, or say, anything that might be considered…inappropriate?"

"Not really—" I stop midsentence.

Ryan leans in. "What?"

I feel my cheeks turn red. "Just one time. Modern got canceled because Quentin had the flu, so I got home earlier than usual. Mom was still working days, but she got stuck at the hospital because the second-shift nurse was running late. When I showed up at the apartment, Andrew was there."

"He had keys by then," Mr. Ryan states, almost to himself. "Okay, so what did Andrew do when you showed up?"

"Not much. It's just, after today—" Out loud, it sounds ridiculous.

"Go on," he urges. "Anything could help."

I stare at the napkin holder. "When I came in, Andrew was folding laundry."

"His laundry?" Jacy asks.

I wish I were someplace, anyplace else, instead of at a table with two guys. "*My* laundry. My, like, private laundry. He said he was helping Mom out but you know, a man touching your private stuff is…"

A vision of the doll fills my brain.

"Sorry, Alicia," Mr. Ryan says. "I know that's upsetting, but no judge in the country will issue a subpoena because a guy was folding laundry. Do you have any other evidence? Anything at all?"

Jacy and I exchange another look. It's been the problem all along. We haven't found real proof for anyone.

Ryan takes the silence as an answer. "Did Andrew give you the key as soon as you asked for it?"

"Yes. But he could have made a copy before that, right?"

The helplessness in my voice is easy to hear. Perhaps that's what makes Mr. Ryan decide to take action.

"Get me his address. I'd like to meet this Andrew fellow myself."

chapter thirty-seven

Two days later, about half an hour after Mom leaves for work, the outside call button screeches. When I ask who's there, a tinny voice announces, "Ryan." I buzz him in and text Jacy. By the time Mr. Ryan gets out of the elevator, Jacy's waiting with me.

Mr. Ryan nods approvingly at the brightly lit living room, the closed venetian blinds.

"Had a little chat with your Mr. Thomson." Mr. Ryan settles into the wing chair across from the couch. "He won't bother you anymore."

"Ali's right?" Jacy asks. "Andrew's the stalker?"

"Well…" Mr. Ryan's hand turns in a sort of wavering gesture. "He didn't actually confess. It's not like TV. Perps rarely do."

"Then how do you know it's him?" I ask.

"Have you ever been inside his apartment?" Mr. Ryan asks. I shake my head.

"Cameras, pornography…pictures of you all over the place—"

I can't help but shudder as I think about the times I was alone with Andrew.

"What about the smell?" Jacy asks. "Did you notice a peculiar smell in any of the rooms?"

Ryan gives him an odd look. "What are you talking about?"

"We forgot to tell you. I smelled a kind of woodsy smell. Like incense. Or maybe some kind of clove cigarette. Twice. Once when the guy broke in to Ali's bedroom after the Baltimore trip, then again at the concert. After the lights went out."

Mr. Ryan turns a questioning eye to me.

"I never smelled it. I wasn't in the audience and if it was in my bedroom, it was very faint—"

"You never told me that." Jacy pouts.

"It's not that I didn't believe you. Obviously, you have a better sense of smell than I do."

"There wasn't any unusual odor in Mr. Thomson's apartment, but it would have been nice to know ahead of time." Ryan shakes out a mint with more than a little displeasure. "Really, kids, you should have told me when it happened. There's this survivalist guy who lives under the bridge…"

I pick at the hole in my jeans. "You're right. Sorry, I've been so stressed-out."

Jacy, however, is not in an apologetic mode. "What does it matter? You just said the stalker's Andrew. Unless you got it wrong—"

"I didn't," Ryan snaps. "Andrew's the perp."

"Did he explain himself?" Jacy asks. "Like why he started stalking Ali now? After all those months of going out with her mom—"

"It has nothing to do with Mrs. Ruffino. Like I said, Mr.

Thomson didn't own up to it all, but he did admit to watching those videos your friend shot. My assumption is he started thinking about Alicia in a different way." Ryan's eyes flash as he turns to me. "It's not surprising you're stressed-out. It was a very stupid thing to do. The internet is so much more dangerous than any of you kids ever think it is. You put personal profiles on websites, upload all kinds of footage—and then wonder why you lose privacy. You wouldn't keep your front door unlocked, would you?"

I shake my head.

"Of course not. But you have no problem dancing around like crazy, opening that window to the world—"

I want to melt into the furniture. I pray that Mr. Ryan won't break his promise and tell Mom. She'd be just as furious.

Jacy, however, is thinking logically. "How do you know Andrew'll stop?"

Mr. Ryan gives us the steely-eyed, "I'll slam you against the wall if you don't cooperate" cop glare. "Because he'll have to deal with me if he comes within two miles of here. Our Mr. Thomson assured me he understood. I *made* him assure me."

Jacy nods. "That'll work. Because I wouldn't want to mess with you, either."

chapter thirty-eight

The last day of school before winter vacation is a half day. Clarissa, Sonya and I stop at Tony's for lunch and then split up. I continue down Montague. Finally! Time for a little Christmas shopping.

I'm on my way to the thrift shop to see if I can score a couple of good gifts when Samantha screeches out of Starbucks. "Ali? Ruffino! Wait up!"

I stop just to quiet her down.

"Where've you been?" she demands.

"Around…"

"Quentin had to re-block the dance, you know. Are you going to switch studios?"

I scrape the sidewalk with a toe. "I'm not dancing anymore."

Samantha's brown eye widens so that it almost matches the blue one for size. "Because of Cisco?"

"Excuse me?"

"Cisco and Eva," she says. "Because of what happened."

"I have no idea what you're talking about."

"You really are a slut." She laughs. "Hooking up with Cisco—"

"Are you crazy? I didn't—"

"Oh, come on. I saw him leave the studio that night."

"What night?"

"Auditions. He came out the side and then it took you forever to open the front door. You looked all spaced-out. I didn't get it at first. Then Eva dumped his ass as soon as Winter Fest was over, and I put two and two together. Did you do it in the dressing room? The studio?"

"Sam—"

Her motormouth keeps right on revving. "Doesn't matter. I figured Eva must have found out what happened and reamed you out right before your solo. That's why you freaked—"

"I freaked because someone was stalking me."

Samantha blinks. "You mean *dancergirl*'s real? There's an actual *shyboy?*"

I pull her into the alley so no one on the street can hear. "No, not *shyboy*. Blake was right. It was one of my friends. But then this…pervert started taping me in my bedroom. Without me knowing. *Then* he shows up at the concert and uploads the solo. Don't tell me you didn't see it."

Samantha shifts her weight awkwardly.

You saw it! You watched a thousand times, laughed your head off. Must have been hard not to pick up the phone to gloat about the fact that you didn't think I deserved it in the first place.

"That's why I'm quitting. Not because of Cisco and Eva."

Sam looks stricken. "Then you should come back."

Something about her look makes me wonder if it's happening to her, too. If somehow Andrew discovered Sam because of me. When he went to the show, he would have seen her.

"You don't have to worry," I say. "The guy's not doing it anymore—"

"There is no guy."

I stare at her. "What does that mean, 'There is no guy'?"

"Maybe there is a guy, but he didn't put the solo on Zube."

"Of course he did—"

Her voice is barely above a whisper. "I did it."

"Excuse me?"

"I put the solo online. My folks taped the concert..." Samantha blinks. "It was a joke, okay? *Dancergirl* was already on the net. How was I supposed to know it would make you quit?"

"Are you kidding? Like it wouldn't totally embarrass me—"

"You didn't seem embarrassed dancing in your panties," she shoots back.

"That was private! It's what I'm trying to tell you! Some perv shot secret video of me in my bedroom!"

She puts a hand on her hip. "Really? Oh, really? I'm sorry, Ali. I didn't know."

That's when I totally lose it. I keep my voice down, but there is no doubting my fury. "You know something, Sam? If I hadn't already left Moving Arts, I'd do it right this second. Who wants to be in the same studio as you?"

When I get home, Mom's note is propped up on the kitchen table: "Shopping before my shift."

I beep to let her know I'm home, then text Jacy.

Something new. Can you talk?

His reply comes quickly. Almost home. I'll come to u.

He gets there about fifteen minutes later. He's wearing black jeans, a long-sleeved pullover and his jacket. He takes off his sunglasses.

We automatically head to my bedroom where I tell him about Samantha.

"Just because Sam uploaded the solo doesn't mean Andrew wasn't responsible for the rest," Jacy says. "It's a coincidence, that's all."

"Not really."

"What's that supposed to mean?" he asks.

"Every single thing that happened this year is because of *dancergirl*."

"Oh, come on. Don't let Mr. Ryan's stupid lecture get to you. You had every right to do *dancergirl*. It's putting the solo online that's wrong. No matter how jealous Sam is—and that's what this is about—it's a sucky thing to do."

"I know. But still, it's my fault."

"Ali—"

"You don't understand! I liked it at first. Liked being the center of attention, liked everyone thinking I'm cool!"

"There's nothing wrong with that."

"There is. I was…tempting fate or something."

Jacy sags back into the bed. "Maybe things would be different if I'd gone back to Irving."

"You have to go to this other school."

He picks at my quilt. "Not really. I could have stayed at WiHi, then gone to an after-school program. Mom gave me the choice."

The thought that he chose to go to McAllister is mind-blowing. "Why would you want to leave WiHi if you didn't have to?"

"Because I can't bear the thought of everyone finding out about my eyes. Feeling sorry for me. All the 'There goes the blind kid.'"

"Nobody would—"

Jacy pounds the wall. "Exactly. Nobody would *say* anything. But I know what they'd think. 'Poor Jacy. His life is ruined—'"

"Would you stop? Your life isn't ruined!" I shift my body so that I can look directly into his eyes. "You're the most amazing person I know. That any of us knows. The smartest person in the room, always, but you don't show off. You've never once made anyone feel stupid or like they're one millimeter less than you. You're a math whiz, a writing genius, interested in, like, everything—and the best friend any human being can have. Even if you do have totally crazy hair. And I *know* you're going to do great things with your life, Jace. RP can't stop you. I won't let it—"

That's when it happens. I'm not sure how. Maybe I pull Jacy toward me, maybe he leans in—but the next thing I know, Jeremy Carl Strode and I are locked in an embrace. Lips, and then tongues, press together...

chapter thirty-nine

The simultaneous ringing of cell phones pulls us apart.

"Sorry," I mumble.

"I didn't mean—"

"Forget it. Didn't happen," I say.

Jacy takes the call while I hurry out of the bedroom. By the time I reach my phone, lying on the coffee table, the call has gone to voice mail. Just as well. I don't want to talk to anyone, including Clarissa.

I busy myself in the living room. Fold a wrinkled sweater, stack the newspaper Mom left in scattered sections. When Jacy enters, I can't look at him.

"I think I'll see if Mr. Ryan is home. Tell him about Samantha. Maybe we're wrong about Andrew. Maybe he should talk to that survivalist guy—"

"Sure, but I mean, I thought we were going to forget what just happened."

"We are," I hurry to say. "I just figured you wouldn't want to talk to Ryan right now."

"I do. I mean, if you do. Unless you don't want me to."

"I do. We can go together."

"Okay. Give me half an hour. I've got to deal with something."

It's too awkward to ask what it is.

"Meet in the lobby at, like, 2:45," he says.

After he leaves, my mind spins. What on earth happened? Who started it? Does it even matter? It's a mistake. Jacy and I know everything about each other. My ChapStick fetish, his no underwear. Ohhh! My face gets warm at the thought of Jacy naked.

I return Clarissa's call but don't tell her what happened. Sometimes, you've got to resist the urge to give TMI. Otherwise, I'd have blurted out the fact that Jeremy Carl Strode is a rather excellent kisser.

Jacy's on the stoop by the time I get downstairs.

"Nice out," I say, because it's better than the old "How about dem Yankees?" my Tío uses whenever he wants to avoid something. Especially since the Yankees don't play in winter and Tío Marcos never *kissed* the person—for the very first time—just thirty minutes before.

"Crazy," Jacy mumbles. "Freezing in November. Spring in late December."

"Global warming. I don't get how some people refuse to believe it's happening!"

Jacy starts to talk about his weather-related computer project. I don't ask about his partners. If one of them is *quiksilver,* I don't want to know.

We reach the deli. I glance into the plateglass window. Mr. Ryan's wedged into the back booth that practically has his name etched into the leather. His plate's pushed to the side, coffee cup drained. He has on tiny white earbuds and gazes intently at his laptop.

The restaurant is nearly empty. Doris, behind the counter, sets racks of clean glasses onto shelves. They clatter so much it's a wonder the glass doesn't shatter.

"Mr. Ryan!" Jacy says. "Just the person we're looking for."

Ryan, wearing a blue-and-green lumberman's shirt, snaps down the computer lid. His earbuds tangle and one pulls out of his ear.

"Sorry we startled you." I'm about to tell him about Samantha when Jacy's fingers dig into my arm. His face turns street-mime white.

"You okay?" I ask.

He shoots me a look I can't read. "Dizzy…"

He plops onto the leather banquette opposite Mr. Ryan.

"Did you eat anything?" That's the first thing Mom asks whenever I feel weird.

Jacy nods.

"Put your head down," Mr. Ryan advises.

Jacy does as he's told. After a while, he looks at me. "I must be coming down with something. We should go back home."

"Sure," I say. "But—"

Jacy jerks me toward the door. "Come on, Ali! I really feel sick!"

"Slow down. Especially if you're dizzy. You'll trip."

He forces himself to walk slower. "Don't look back."

"Why? What's wrong? Did something happen with your eyes—"

He pulls me to the sidewalk, then into the alley. Safe behind a Dumpster, Jacy glances back. No one's there.

"Would you please tell me what's going on?" I whisper.

"Did you hear what was playing on Ryan's laptop?"

"Excuse me?"

"When the earbud fell out," Jacy says. "He shut the computer but it caught on the cable—"

"Okay…?"

"Did you hear anything?"

I shake my head. "Doris was making too much noise—"

"The Clash," Jacy says.

My breath gets stuck at *pause*. "Are you sure?"

"Never been so sure of anything in my life. It was your song, the one from the concert."

"That doesn't mean anything. It could be a coincidence."

Jacy shakes his head. "You're the one who said there aren't any coincidences. Did you notice how fast he shut the laptop when he saw us?"

"We startled him."

"Oh, we startled him all right. He was watching you dance on the screen and then, poof, you appear in front of his face."

I lean against the brick wall. My turn to be dizzy—only it isn't an act. "What about Andrew?"

"Ryan trapped us. Asked enough questions until it appeared that *someone* you know was the guy. Bet he never even talked to him. Probably made up all that stuff about Andrew's apartment." Jacy's eyes widen. "That's why he was so pissed about the smell. He would have blamed the survivalist guy if we told him about it. A lot less work than making it seem like it's Andrew."

"Hold on." It's hard to think straight. "Even if Ryan taped the concert, I never finished the dance. The music stopped in the middle."

"Exactly. But I sat there with my head on the table for a couple of minutes, right? The song played out and then started again. Which means he wasn't watching you at the concert.

He was watching you rehearse in your bedroom. He has stuff he didn't put on the net, Ali. Video he keeps just for him-self—"

Omigod! I remember the paranoid feeling I had when I was with Luke. This feels exactly the same. Still...

"You didn't see the screen, Jacy. We can't know for sure it's Ryan. Did you ever smell that woodsy smell when we talked to him? I haven't. Not once."

Jacy's grip on my arm tightens. "Let's go back."

"To the deli?"

"Yeah. I'll say I feel better. You tell him about Sam."

"Why?"

"Because I want to see if I can get into his computer," Jacy says. "Maybe he'll use the bathroom. Or go up front and pay the bill. Then I can check the hard drive. See if there's foot-age of you."

"What if we get caught?" Nervous, I smear my lips with ChapStick.

"If you don't want to do it, that's fine. I'll go myself."

He takes off but I can't let him face that guy alone. "Wait up! I'm coming!"

When we get to the deli, I glance at the window.

Ryan's booth is empty.

chapter forty

Jacy's arm is on mine as we head down the street. He's determined to get into Ryan's apartment.

"Same plan as before. I'll say I feel better. You explain about Samantha and I'll try to find out where he leaves his computer."

"This is crazy—" I begin.

Up ahead, a middle-aged woman exits Ryan's building. I scoot up the stairs, politely hold the outer door for her so I can catch the inner one before it shuts. Jacy follows me in.

It's a typical Heights brownstone. Two apartments on each floor. Old-fashioned wall sconces attached to the striped olive-and-tan wallpaper make it possible to see in the otherwise dim hallway. At least I can see.

Jacy blinks. Directly ahead of us is a solid maple stairway. A green runner, like a sluggish river, rolls down the middle of the steps.

"It's here!" he whispers.

As soon as he says it, I know what he means. The hall has a definite smell. Woodsier than either clove or patchouli. A field trip to the natural history museum springs to mind. Sage. Used in Native American rituals.

A door above us opens.

Jacy and I freeze. One look at my face and Ryan will know I know. We have to get away—but the brownstone's front doors are made of wood and etched glass. Ryan will see us running down the stoop. That's when Cisco flashes into my mind. He entered the studio through the back door. I grab Jacy's arm.

Footsteps have started down the steps. We'll never make it out the back in time. I push Jacy into a small recess under the stairwell, force myself in beside him.

Did Ryan see us from his window? Does he know we're here?

The blood in my ears pounds so hard I'm sure it can be heard.

The person coming down the steps halts for a moment, then goes for the front door. I wait a few seconds before getting up and peeking out the door window. Through the glass I see Mr. Ryan, carrying a gym bag, walk down the stoop.

"He's gone," I whisper.

"Time to call in the cavalry," Jacy says. "We've got to get better proof that Ryan did it than just some smell in a hallway. We need help pronto!"

chapter forty-one

Back in Jacy's room, Charlie paces. "There's a camera in your bedroom, Ali. Has to be. That's how the guy got footage of you rehearsing your solo."

"Damn! Not just that!" I fumble through my messenger bag, find the note from the florist and toss it on the bed. "Check out the first line. That's what threw me the night of the concert. At first, I thought you sent the sunflowers, Jacy."

Charlie reads, "'Seize the moment.' Sounds like Strode, for sure. Guess the dude wanted Ali to suspect you, Ace."

"Asshole!" Jacy exclaims.

Charlie sits at the desk, types something on Jacy's laptop.

I peer over his shoulder. "What are you doing?"

"He must not be using a regular camera, or you'd have seen it. Has to be a nanny cam. You know, the kind that comes inside a teddy bear so parents can spy on the babysitter."

"I'd have noticed an extra stuffed animal in my room. I don't have that many."

"Maybe there's one that looks like something you already have." Charlie leans back. "Check it out."

I scroll through the photos. "These are too new. Mine are all ratty...."

Jacy thinks. "So he took one of your old ones, hollowed it out and hid a camera inside. He had plenty of time during your Baltimore trip."

Baltimore.

"What?" Jacy asks me.

"It feels like I'm missing something. Something important."

Jacy and Charlie exchange glances.

"Think about it logically," Jacy says. "Like a math problem. Step by step."

"Okay. Wouldn't a camera have to be plugged in? No camera has a battery that lasts longer than a few hours."

Charlie's eyes gleam behind his glasses. "Good! What's plugged in where?"

I stare at Jacy's stuff and imagine my room. "The computer on the desk. Printer. Lamps. The one next to the door and the one by my bed— Omigod!"

"What?"

"My clock radio. The day after we got back from Baltimore, I overslept because the alarm was set for p.m., not a.m. I had no idea how that happened but— What are you doing?"

Charlie's already pulled up a different spy-cam site. "Do any of these look like your alarm clock?"

I stare at the screen. "The second one. But how—"

"Ryan is one lucky perv. You have the same radio a million other people have. This company takes the five most popular types and puts cameras in them."

"How would Ryan know what kind I have? I told you. I pulled the blinds down right after I started working on the solo—"

Charlie points to Jacy's window. "When he first taped your

bedroom from the fire escape, he would have gotten the clock on video. Maybe he didn't notice it then, but after you closed the blinds, he reviews the tapes, looking for some place to hide a camera. He sees the clock, checks online like I did. He buys the spy-cam version and switches it with yours. Voilà—a direct feed from your room."

"How did he know we'd be gone for the whole weekend? He'd need time to break in. With Mom asleep in the day, and me home at night, our apartment has someone there almost 24/7."

"Who knows? Maybe he chatted up your mom on the street and found out about the trip." Charlie shrugs. "The point is—he got in. The only mistake he made was to set the alarm to p.m., not a.m."

"What do we do now? Go to the police?"

"We should check the clock to see if Charlie's right," Jacy says.

"Won't Ryan know we're onto him?" I ask. "At the very least, he'll figure out that we know *someone's* taping me. I mean, unless we make it seem like we think it's Andrew."

Jacy stops midstep. "We can do that. Or we can knock the plug out—" he makes quotes with his fingers "—*accidentally.* Check it quick, plug it back in. As long as we don't say anything about Ryan when we're in the room, there's no way he'll know we're onto him."

It isn't until Charlie shows me the camera lens, disguised as a dial in the front of the clock radio, that the truth sinks in. I stagger to the kitchen and collapse into a chair, trying to sort through it all.

"I still don't get how it works. The camera in the clock radio tapes me in my bedroom but how does Ryan see it? Is he breaking in to the apartment on a regular basis, changing tapes?" A shudder ripples my body. "Does he sneak in when Mom's asleep?"

"He doesn't have to," Charlie says. "Once he got the spy cam set up, he doesn't have to break in again *if* he's feeding the footage into a wireless network. Like at the video store— Oh, man!"

"What?" Jacy and I ask at the same time.

"Do you know your block's under surveillance?" Charlie asks. "I noticed a camera on a streetlamp when I was walking over here. I assumed it was one of those traffic cams the city uses to catch cars speeding through red lights. But, really, now that I think about it, they only do that at major intersections."

My head hurts. "Mr. Ryan told me he was watching the street but I thought he meant from the stoop or his window."

"He's doing a lot more than staring out a window," Jacy mutters.

"If we go to the cops with the alarm clock, can we get him arrested?" I ask.

Charlie looks grim. "I'm not so sure. The cops are his friends, right? Why should they believe it's him, unless…"

"What?" Jacy asks.

"We turn the tables." Charlie thinks for a moment before pumping a fist into the air. "Oh, yeah! In just a little while we are going to get verifiable proof that Mr. Whatever His First Name Is Ryan is a major sleazeball."

chapter forty-two

Charlie's plan is diabolical in its symmetry. An "elegant solution," as Mr. Han might say. Get into the brownstone and onto the fire escape, and then videotape Ryan's apartment through his very own window. Charlie's pretty sure he'll find something incriminating that we can go to the cops with.

He always carries a camera. Charlie pulls it out of his backpack and checks the batteries. "Ryan's probably got the street cam running to a monitor. I'm sure that's illegal. Violation of some constitutional amendment, right, Ace?"

Jacy's thinking about something else. "It's a good idea, Charlie, but we can't do it when Ryan's home. He left when Ali and I were there, but he could be back by now. How long will it take?"

"Not long. I'll do a long-shot pan, then close-up on anything that's interesting. Three, maybe four minutes."

"Okay. But we need to make sure he's gone."

"I got that one," I say. It's surreal the way the plan's falling into place. "After school one day, Ryan gave me both his landline and cell numbers in case of emergency. Took mine, too, the creep. I'll call his apartment. If he's there, I'll ask him to meet us at the deli. Then I'll tell him about Samantha while Charlie gets inside the building. And if he's not home now, we're good, right?"

We look at each other. Calculate.

"One more thing," Charlie says. "Just in case. Do you have a flashlight?"

Jacy nods. He returns with three.

"I only need one," Charlie says.

"Can't hurt to have extras," Jacy explains.

It's winter solstice, the shortest day of the year. By five o'clock, it'll be too dark for Jacy to see, so I know that's why he wants the light.

When we get out onto the street, Charlie turns right.

"Wrong way," I say. "Ryan lives—"

"I know what I'm doing."

He leads us down Clinton. We turn onto Remsen Street and follow him to China Express.

"You're kidding, right?" I breathe. "You're hungry?"

"Keep cool. One fried rice," he tells the elderly woman behind the counter. "For takeout."

When it comes, he makes me pay the $3.95. Then he uses the woman's stapler to clip the bill to the brown paper bag. Once we're outside, he pulls a pencil from his backpack.

"Can you please tell me what you're doing?" I ask.

"In a minute. What's Ryan's address?"

"484 Clinton."

Charlie writes 482 followed by a couple of Chinese letters. I lean over. "You know Chinese?"

Charlie laughs. "Not according to my parents. That says '482 Happy New Year' but no one'll know the difference when the 'delivery boy' shows up. I don't want to waste time on the street hoping someone comes out of the building like you guys did before."

"But nobody actually ordered Chinese. How do you think you're getting in?"

"Come on, Ali. We live in Home Delivery Heights. Groceries, drugstore, pizza. I'll keep hitting buttons until somebody buzzes me in. Bet it doesn't take three seconds."

Jacy gives Charlie the WiHi handshake and they laugh. "Brilliant!"

"It's only brilliant if we don't get caught," I mutter. "This guy was a cop and a crazy one. Don't forget that."

"That's why I took a flashlight. If I get into trouble on the fire escape, I'll flash twice."

I groan. "Who do you think you are? Batman?"

Charlie shrugs. "I watch a lot of movies."

"Yeah, well, you can also use your cell. And while I remember, put it on silent. You don't want it to ring when you're out there."

As if to prove my point, Charlie's cell vibrates just as we get near Clinton Street.

"Clarissa found Sonya," he tells us. "They're in place."

"In place?"

"Thought we needed a few extras. I called Clarissa just before we left Jacy's. Told her to get Sonya."

"Charlie, I'm glad you're helping," I say, "but this isn't a movie! It's real life. Dangerous real life."

"Chill. Time to call Ryan."

My hand shakes as I find Ryan's number in my cell. He doesn't pick up the landline.

"Excellent. He's still out." Charlie puts his phone on speaker so Sonya and Clarissa can hear. "The girls wait on Montague. As soon as you two see me, start walking down Clinton. Jacy and Ali come from this end. I'll get into the building with my delivery, and you four 'accidentally' run into each other in front of Ryan's building. Start chatting, sit on the steps. If he comes home before I get out, go to the deli, talk to him on the stoop, whatever. Just don't let him inside the brownstone until I'm out."

"Do we really have to go through all this?" I ask.

"He's got the street wired, Ali. What if we don't find anything right now? You don't want him getting suspicious if he checks the footage."

"Yeah, okay, I get it. But what if you need help? One of us should go with you."

Jacy nods. "After you get buzzed in, don't close the door all the way. I'll slip inside."

That is the worst idea I've heard so far.

"No way, Jace. He's using the *roof* to get down the fire escape." I remember, even if he doesn't, the night on our building. "Jacy's afraid of heights, Charlie. I'll go."

All of a sudden, this is more than a good idea. It's a "gotcha." My revenge for all the crap Ryan put me through.

"Don't even think about arguing. What if someone from another building sees Charlie on the fire escape and calls the cops? If I'm there, I'll tell them Ryan's stalking me. Even if they don't believe it, they'll have to investigate. So we get what we want no matter what happens."

"What if Mr. Ryan wonders why you're not with me?" Jacy counters.

For the first time this afternoon, I grin. "You're the genius. I have full confidence in your ability to figure out something logical to tell him."

"You win." Jacy sighs. "Ali goes, too."

"Whatever. Time's a-wasting." Charlie slings his backpack

over his shoulder. "Don't forget to position yourself so one of you looks at the building in case Ali or I use the flashlight."

Charlie gets to the brownstone about half a minute before Jacy and I run into Clarissa and Sonya. He presses a buzzer. No answer. From the corner of my eye, I watch him hit another, then a third button. A few seconds later, an elderly voice comes through the speaker.

"Who is it?"

"Delivery," Charlie calls.

"That was fast. I only called it in ten minutes ago."

Charlie shows great restraint by not turning around to give us an "I told you so" wink. After the woman buzzes Charlie in, the rest of us move to the stoop. I quietly slip through the door Charlie left slightly ajar.

"Sorry, ma'am, I'm not from the Rite Aid." Charlie's voice, echoing from the second floor, sounds like he's talking to a deaf person.

"I didn't order Chinese," the old woman insists.

"Someone did. That's okay. I'll find them. You go back inside."

Charlie stomps to the third floor. As soon as the woman's door closes, I scoot up two flights of steps. At the end of the hallway, a short staircase leads to a metal door. Charlie's already there.

"No good," he tells me.

Unlike our roof, there's no push bar. This door has a lock that's locked.

"It's okay," I whisper. "The first floor has a backyard entrance. We can try from there. But be quiet. I don't want everyone to hear us running through the building."

He treads lightly down the steps. On the first floor, I glance out toward the stoop. Jacy and Sonya sit on the steps talking, Clarissa leans against the railing. She looks up casually, on flashlight duty.

I catch up to Charlie. He grins—the back door has a dead bolt that he's unlocked. Just before he goes through, I pull his jacket.

"What if someone's out there?"

Charlie holds up the takeout. "Gotta deliver or I don't get a tip." He steps into the garden, looks around. "All clear!"

The apartments on the ground floor have built-in metal bars on the windows, but there aren't any on the upper floors. Just like we expected, there's a fire escape. But the ladder that leads from Ryan's second-floor landing to the ground is hooked onto the platform. That prevents exactly what Charlie and I want to do—climb *up*.

He checks to see if there's a regular ladder or chair that we can stand on to get to Ryan's landing, but it's December. Everything that might have been out there is stored in the basement.

Charlie looks crushed. I hold up my hand to tell him to hold on. I calculate the height of the platform. I'm almost sure my plan will work.

Moving close to the fire escape, I explain how to perform a lift. "You have to bend your knees, Charlie, so you don't get hurt. When I tell you, lift me from my hips. I'll do the rest." As we get into position, I say, "Make sure to work with my timing!"

I plié. Charlie bends and puts his arms around my hips. "Now!"

At the same time Charlie boosts me, I jump so as to get more height. I raise my arms into first position. Fingers brush the second-floor rail, but I can't quite grab hold. I tumble to the ground.

"Almost," I gasp. "Try again. A little higher. Big breath."

This time, my fingers get a decent grip on the metal. I swing for a few seconds. When I have enough momentum, I contract my stomach muscles, point my feet hard and tuck my legs in and over the top of the rail. Like a gymnast, I flip onto the fire-escape platform.

"Whoa!" Charlie whispers. "Wish I'd gotten that down on tape."

I manage a brief smile as I unhook the ladder and let it down as quietly as I can. "*Dancergirl* and *shyboy*—together at last. Just not the way anyone imagined."

Charlie climbs onto the fire escape, and then it's his turn. He hands me the delivery bag, slips the camera out of his backpack and looks into the window. It's curtained, although the striped blue fabric has been pushed aside to allow light.

"Damn," Charlie whispers.

It's a picture-perfect bedroom. Bed made military-style, clothes put away, not a shoe out of place. The problem for us is that there isn't a hint of electronics.

"He's got to have the stuff in another room," Charlie insists.

The fire escape fronts only the one bedroom, so we can't check the other windows. Disappointed, I'm about to give up and climb back down when Charlie points to the sill. The window's cracked about an inch.

"No way. You are not going to break in to his apartment."

"Didn't come this far…" He begins to lift the pane and then stops. "The guy doesn't have a dog, does he? I don't hear barking but—"

"No dog. I'd have seen Ryan walking him. Besides, most of the brownstones around here don't allow pets."

"Cool." He puts one leg over the sill. "You don't have to come in if you don't want to."

Right. Give the neighbors more time to see me on the fire escape. "It's safer inside than out."

I slip into Ryan's bedroom. Just being in the apartment creeps me out so bad I have to stop to breathe. "Go ahead, Charlie. I'll call the guys and let them know what we're doing."

Nervous, I hit Clarissa's number instead of Jacy's.

"No sign of Ryan," she tells me. "But be careful! Breaking and entering isn't part of the plan."

Don't I know it!

I move quickly into the living room. It's as neat as Ryan's bedroom. Except for an old television, however, it's empty of both electronics—and humans.

"Charlie?" I whisper-call.

"Back here."

A second bedroom is across the hall. I move inside and gasp.

"Told you," he says.

It's the pictures that first catch my attention. Uniformed men, soldiers and cops, are pinned all over the walls. A couple of guard dogs sneer down at us. A pile of Neighborhood Watch signs is stacked in the corner. Someone might be comforted by all that...*watchfulness,* but it looks like obsession to me.

Charlie's already panning the walls with his camera. I step out of the way, move to the equipment set up on Ryan's desk.

It takes a moment to register what I'm looking at. When it does, I can barely speak.

I wet my lips. "Charlie..."

He takes one look at my face and hustles over. He whistles.

The monitor centered on the desk is split into four "screens." One quadrant shows the view from the street cam. The second is focused on the front of my building. The last two are views of my bedroom.

The floor spins in front of me. For a second, I'm afraid I'm going to be sick. Seeing *my* room on the monitor in *his* room is beyond disgusting. Creepier than any nightmare—

"Unreal," Charlie says, snapping me back to reality.

He checks out the rest of the equipment on the desk. A black box sits under the monitor. Buttons are on the left, a joystick to the right. Charlie moves the joystick and immediately the street-cam screen changes view. "That's what I thought. He can follow anyone up, or down, the street."

Ryan watched me coming, going and in my room.

Seized by paranoia worse than anything I've ever felt, I grab Charlie's arm. "Move it back to where it was. He can't know we were here."

Charlie fiddles with the joystick and the screen reverts to its original view. Then he picks up his camera, and begins to shoot close-ups of the desk and monitor.

My cell rings. Charlie looks up, startled. I'd warned him to put his on vibrate, but had forgotten to do the same.

"Sorry," I tell him. I speak into the phone. "What's up?"

"Ryan's coming down the block," Sonya says.

"Damn! Charlie, he's coming back."

"Stick with the plan," Charlie says. "Tell them to get Ryan to the deli."

I relay the message.

"We know," Sonya says. "Just wanted to warn you. Get out of there quick, Ali. I don't like this—"

"Me, neither." I hang up and immediately switch my phone to silent. "Enough, Charlie. Let's go—"

"Just a minute." He's opening desk drawers, rifling through DVD boxes.

"What are you looking for—"

This time, my cell vibrates.

Clarissa. Totally panicked. "He went into the building. Said he has to drop off his gym bag. He'll meet us—"

"Charlie! He's coming. Wants to drop off a bag—" I freeze at the sound of the front door being unlocked.

I stare at Charlie, terrified.

He puts a finger to his lips and points to the closet. It's the only place we could possibly hide. I pray the door won't squeak.

It doesn't. The only thing that hangs in the closet is a leather jacket, although plenty of boxes are stacked on the floor. There's barely enough room for Charlie and me to squeeze in. He grabs the door's painted edge, but the knob is on the outside. The door doesn't completely close.

I pray Ryan drops the gym bag in the living room. Then he can leave the apartment, walk to the deli…

Footsteps move down the hall. They cross into the other bedroom. Okay, fine. He'll drop off the bag in there—no! He's already out and crossing into this room. My palms are sweaty with fear. *Omigod!* A horrible realization strikes. I'm not holding the Chinese-food delivery bag.

Did I drop it in his bedroom when I climbed in? That would explain why Ryan's in here.

My eyes focus on the thin slice of air between the door and the frame. When Ryan crosses into view, I glance down like a little kid playing hide-n-seek.

If I don't see you, you can't see me.

A fist pounds the apartment door.

"Mr. Ryan?" Jacy calls. "We're waiting."

Ryan grunts, drops the gym bag and exits. My knees tremble with relief. The front door slams. Charlie and I tumble from the cramped closet.

"That was close," he whispers. "Plus, it smelled so bad in there I was afraid I'd gag."

Charlie's right. I was so scared, it hadn't penetrated that the closet stinks—the same smell Jacy discovered. I'm not sure if it came from the one of the boxes or the jacket but I don't care.

"We are so gone, Charlie."

Just as we get to the doorway, I glance back to make sure everything's the same as when we came in. That's when I see the delivery bag. I'd dropped it beside the desk. Charlie gives me a horrified look as I scoop it up. Then we rush into the other bedroom to find yet another shock. We'd left the window wide open!

When we get to ground level, I hit Clarissa's number.

"Where are you?" she asks.

"In the yard. Is it safe to leave the building?"

Clarissa raises her voice. "It's Ali." She lowers it. "We just got to the deli. Jacy'll tell Ryan about Samantha, so don't come here. Meet back at your place."

It isn't until Charlie and I are in my living room that my breath returns to something even close to normal.

chapter forty-three

Everyone talks at once until Jacy puts a stop to it. One by one, we go over what happened—the stuff we saw in the back bedroom, the way Ryan insisted he had to go upstairs to drop off the bag, how lucky it was that Jacy pounded on the door when he did. And exactly how many times Ryan asked Jacy when he thought I would show up.

"I told him you had to buy rice and a bunch of other stuff at the market for your mom," Jacy says. "And then you had to bring it here, so it might take a while."

"The guy creeped me out so bad, I'm still shaking." Clarissa shudders. "He had this look when Jacy told him about Samantha. I thought he was going to rush right out and break her neck."

"Wouldn't surprise me. You should see his place. All those pictures of guards and dogs on the walls." Charlie stands. "Okay. I'll go back to my house and burn a couple of DVDs so Ali can take one to the police station."

"Cool," Jacy says. "Charlie, makes copies and— What's wrong?"

Charlie's checked his cell. "Damn, Ace. I was supposed to be at work half an hour ago. I can make copies there, although I don't get out until eleven. That's kind of late—"

"Police stations don't exactly turn into pumpkins at the stroke of midnight," Sonya observes. "They're open 24/7."

"I'd rather wait for my mom, anyway," I say. "Now that we *finally* have proof I need to tell her first. And have her come with me. The police will take it way more seriously with Mom standing there, treating them to her 'this is important so you best not ignore me' stare."

Jacy laughs. "Ali's right. I've been the recipient of that way too many times."

"What time does your mom get home?" Charlie asks.

"Early tomorrow morning. Even if I leave a message at the nurse's station, she'll never find someone to cover this late, so it doesn't matter when you get out of work."

Sonya shoots up. "Crap! What time is it? My parents are having their holiday blowout and Clarissa promised to play waitress with me."

"I'm so sorry, Ali." Clarissa looks at Sonya. "Maybe I should stay—"

I shake my head. "It's okay. Jacy's here. I'm just lucky you were all around to help, considering it's the first day of vacation."

"Woo-hoo!" Clarissa tries.

I smile. "Go. I'll be fine."

Hugs all around, Merry Christmases, and before you know it I'm alone with Jacy. He makes a face.

"What's wrong?" I ask.

"I have to leave for a little while, too. My weather group's having an online chat."

"Now? Aren't you on vacation?"

"It's my fault. I didn't want the project hanging over me for two weeks, so I insisted we finish it today. We were supposed to do it earlier. Remember when I went downstairs? I had to ask *quiksilver* to move it to, like, ten minutes from now. I can't change it again."

"Use my computer."

He shakes his head. "Data's in mine. We've been collecting it for months. Plus, your connection's too slow. Shouldn't take too long. Do you want to come with me?"

And watch him talk to *quiksilver?* I think not.

"I'll be okay," I say.

"You sure?" Jacy asks. "You don't look so hot."

"I'm fine. It's just…"

"I know." He looks like he wants to say something more. Instead, he turns toward the door. "I'll be back as soon as I can."

I smile. "Thanks. Not just for that but, you know, for everything."

"You would have done the same. It's what friends do." He swivels his head to find, and then unlock, the lock. "Close up right away, okay?"

I turn the lock and think about what he said.

It's what friends do.

And that really is what we are, what we've always been— just friends. The kiss in the bedroom was a crazy mistake in an insane day.

With everything else I have to worry about, it shouldn't be a big deal. But I can't fool myself. Right now, it feels like a very big deal, indeed.

chapter forty-four

My cell chirps about an hour later. Jacy's picture appears along with a text.

Come to the roof. I need you.

Why didn't he tell me he had to go up there one final time to finish the project? I would have kept him company, helped when it got too dark for him to see. Now he's stuck.

In the hall, I take a moment to lock the apartment door. Despite my rush, I'm not about to do anything idiotic. At the top of the roof-access staircase, I hit the push bar and step onto the tar paper.

"Jacy?"

The breeze brushes my face like a ghostly hand. Electricity crackles ominously through overhead lines. The melancholy cry of a saxophone from a nearby apartment sends a shiver down my back.

The bulb over the doorway pools light directly in front of me. Beyond that, the surrounding buildings, satellite dishes and antennae create deep shadows, all the darker when contrasted with the silvery light of a just-rising half-moon.

The wind shifts slightly as I move forward.

"Jacy! Where are you?"

A spiral of smoke drifts from my right. I can just about make out a ring of stones lying on the tar paper. The crack addict's been back, although I don't see him anywhere. Or is the smoke coming from the survivalist? Is that who's been hanging on my roof all this time—

The text message I receive from Jacy at that very moment is more than a little strange: You r it.

Confused, I scan the roof. Steam vents emerge from the asphalt. Mr. Detwiler's wooden pigeon coop takes up the northeast corner. The building's large water tank stands in the center.

I have absolutely no idea where Jacy is.

Just as I open my mouth to call again, the fear that's been bubbling inside breaks to the surface. Jacy would not play stupid games. Not tonight.

I wheel around. *Got to get out of here.* Before I can get inside the building, back to the safety of my locked apartment, someone steps out of the shadows, blocking the doorway so I can't escape.

chapter forty-five

Ryan! The black pants and bomber jacket I saw in his closet make him nearly invisible in the dark.

"Don't be scared," he tells me. "I won't hurt you."

"Where's Jacy?"

Ryan shrugs. "Haven't seen him since the deli."

"He's not on the roof?" Shock cuts through the fear. "How did you get his phone?"

He laughs. "Finders keepers…"

With all the drama, Jacy must have left his cell at the deli. Or Ryan jacked it when Jace wasn't looking. Either way…

He steps closer, but I counter the move.

"No need to be afraid, Alicia. I've watched over you from the street for years—and you never knew it, did you? I saw the way you grew into a beautiful woman." His voice, which at first sounded soft, hardens. "But it got difficult to protect you once those videos went out on the net. I had to figure out a way to stop it."

I cop a tough attitude that I in no way feel. "By dropping a camera in front of my window? Tell me. Where did you stand?" I point to the Clinton Street side. "There? Or a little ways over there!"

I pray he'll step away from the door to show me the specific spot. Then I can make a run for it....

Ryan doesn't even consider moving. "It doesn't matter where I stood, Alicia. All that matters is the plan worked. It hurt me to do it but there you were, shamelessly flaunting yourself to the entire world. You wouldn't stop, either. But as soon as you saw how foolish you looked—no more *dancergirl*." He shakes his head. "Still, the genie was out of the bottle. I needed a better plan to keep you safe. Had to find a way to get the cameras into your room so I could make sure you were tucked into your bed every night. That weekend you and your mother went away. I watched both of you walk down the street with overnight bags—"

The urban-survival rule Mom drummed into me countless times kicks in: *If you think there might be trouble, start screaming and run!*

That's exactly what I do. Shriek, "Help!" and dash toward the fire-escape ladder.

Ryan, however, is just as quick. He darts after me, extending an arm to hook a belt loop with his fingers. He snaps me back. Cups a large, clammy hand around my mouth.

"Not very smart."

He pulls me to his chest. My back touches his body and I instinctively arch forward. He keeps his left hand over my lips. Something hard presses against my waist...

He listens for anyone who might have heard me scream. I know what the chances of that are. If somebody *had* heard and realized it didn't come from a neighbor's TV, they might bother to glance out the window—but wouldn't see anything. They'd look down. Nobody ever remembers the roof.

And Brooklyn nights are filled with so many random noises
anyhow.

Think! Stay calm!

I have my cell. I'll find a way to beep 505. Mom will call…

Somehow, Ryan reads my mind. He gropes my pockets,
pulls out the phone. His jacket stinks of sweat and sage. That's
when I understand what the smell is. It's a ritual. *His* ritual.
Just like those horrible people I read about online. Instead of
making me wear a red dress, it's Ryan who puts on the jacket
and then burns the leaves that turn him into a watchdog. A
sicko guardian. He wore it when he broke in to my bedroom,
wore it to the dance concert—

Something cold is slapped across my mouth. I struggle, try
to pull it off. Ryan grabs my arms, holds them in front of me
and winds more of the silvery electrical tape around my wrists.

He pulls me to the tar-paper-covered ground. I end up
facedown, right cheek pressed into the gritty asphalt. Ryan
lowers himself and covers me with his body.

"I can't share you, Alicia," he whispers. "I had it all under
control. But then those people, hundreds of thousands, started
thinking they know you. Saying things about you that I knew
to be untrue…"

I twist back and forth, trying desperately to wriggle out
from under him. He has me pinned. A glint of something
catches my eyes. A shard of glass, inches away, reflects a bit of
the moon. The shard isn't very big, but it looks sharp.

I *have* to find a way to grab it.

As if in response to my silent plea, something flutters to
my left. City blackbird, or pigeon, nesting on top of the
water tank. Ryan hears the noise, too. Instinctively, he rises
a bit to check it out.

That's when I make my move. I use my toes to roll onto my

shoulder and grab the glass. With a twist, I swing my taped wrists up in a desperate stabbing motion.

I aim for Ryan's eye but scratch his cheek. It's enough for him to rear back.

I scramble to my feet. Race for the doorway.

And he moves diagonally to cut me off. Shifting direction, I head for the closest hiding spot: behind the water tank. Ryan swears but then grows quiet. I can't tell whether he's going left or right around the tank—or if he plans to wait it out on the other side.

My wrists are still wrapped together, though my fingers are free, so I'm able to rip the tape from my lips. But then, just as I open my mouth, at the last moment I decide not to scream. Not only won't it help, it'll make things worse. Ryan will know exactly where I'm standing. He'll get to me way before anyone else can.

Something squeaks. Blackbird. Disturbed for the second time. There's a *whoosh* of wings. Does that mean Ryan's circling the tank from the left? I hesitate—and am rewarded with a slight, metallic *ping*. Yes. The bird startled Ryan and he bumped into the tank....

I rise to half-toe and move right.

Ryan knows how to move quietly, too. After the ping, I don't hear anything else. Did he switch directions? Are we countering each other in some weird water-tank dance, or heading straight into one another's arms?

I decide to keep going. Despite the breeze, sweat trickles down my back.

Step. Listen. Step. Look.

The rush of blood in my ears is so loud I can't hear the bird. Did Ryan get past her?

Ping.

Once again, he bumps into the tank. Good. Still coming from my left, though not as quiet as me.

But he's smarter. I take another step. And there he is, beady eyes staring at the spot he knew I'd come from. He tosses a bunch of mints. A couple of pieces hit the tank—*ping, ping.* One of them hits my chest.

"That little game was fun, Alicia, but I'd like to go back to where we left off."

"No!" Unlike my first scream, there's no mistaking this one for anything but an epic mix of fear and loathing.

"Ali!"

Jacy stands in the roof-access doorway, clearly lit by the overhead bulb.

Immediately, Ryan pulls me into the shadow cast by the tank. He covers my mouth with his hand. I yell anyway, but all that comes out is a muffled groan. Barely audible to anyone more than an inch away—unless your ears are hypersensitive because your eyes aren't.

"Ali!" Jacy swivels his head. "I know you're here!"

Ryan tightens his grip. I stamp on his toes. He gasps, but doesn't release me.

It's enough. Jacy tracks the sound. He stares directly at us, although I know all he really sees is utter darkness.

Or is it?

"Let her go, Ryan," he says.

Nobody moves. It's like a bad rehearsal when the ensemble gets behind the count and the group falters to a stop. But there's no starting over on the roof, only continuation. Or moving in a new direction, which is what Ryan chooses.

He drags me toward the pigeon coop, stopping a few feet from the roof's edge. He holds me tight, but could easily shove me over the edge.

Jacy, however, follows our progress. He walks forward cautiously, sliding one foot across the tar paper, transferring his weight when it's safe, sliding the other foot. Slow going but Jacy doesn't hesitate.

"Let. Ali. Go," he says.

"Well, well, well." Ryan acts like he just noticed we had company. "If it isn't our little blind boy."

"Looking right at our cameraman. Who loves listening in on private conversations," Jacy retorts. "But I'm not blind yet. Not for a bunch of years. Let her go! I'm the one who figured out what you did. Not Ali. If you're mad at anyone, it should be me."

Ryan removes his left hand from my mouth. His right hand, however, holds my upper arm tightly. "Tell him, Alicia. Tell him how I protect you."

"Jace—" So much fear has settled in, I can't make my tongue work.

"It's okay, Ali," Jacy says. "Did he hurt you?"

Yes, I want to cry. "I'm fine. He's got my arm—"

"Okay. She doesn't want you to touch her, Ryan, so let go."

He stiffens. "That's part of the problem. You let this kid tell you what to do, Alicia—"

Mom's second rule roars at me: *If screaming and running don't do it, go for the balls.*

I slam my knee up as hard as I can. Ryan doubles over. Surprised, he releases my arm. Immediately, I dart over to Jacy. Grab his elbow. It's awkward. My wrists are taped, Jacy's off balance. He trips on a steam vent. He falls, taking me with him. By the time I right myself, Ryan's on us.

Jacy, however, refuses to give up. Somehow, he finds a broken antenna. He whips it around, catching Ryan in the nose.

"Run, Ali!" Jacy screams. "Get help!"

But I can't leave. Even if Jacy could see perfectly, he's no match for Ryan. The ex-cop is taller, heavier and trained to hurt people.

It's over in seconds. Ryan twists Jacy's arm until the antenna drops, then pitches it over the edge. The metal rod clatters into the alley six floors below.

"You'll be down there next if you don't behave," Ryan growls.

He pushes Jacy to the edge of the roof, grabs a piece of cable and ties him to the coop.

Then he turns to me. "You're going to behave nicely now, too, aren't you, Alicia? Because if you don't, I'll untie your little friend and off he goes. Every cop knows accidents happen all the time on rooftops...."

Behind Jacy's back, a light flickers. It takes me a moment to realize it's the flashlight he had with him earlier in the day. On, off, on. An SOS signal?

Luckily, Ryan's too busy scaring the bejesus out of me to notice.

"Then again," he continues, "perhaps his death won't be ruled an accident but a different kind of tragedy. Suicide is so sad because it could be prevented. *If only we'd known he was so depressed.* That's what parents always say...."

He's gotten to within inches of my body. Something alerts him and he turns. "What the—"

In seconds, Ryan pounces on Jacy again and wrestles the flashlight away.

"What do you think this is?" He uses the light to smash Jacy across the cheek. "A cartoon adventure—"

I run toward them. "Mr. Ryan, please. Don't hurt him!"

Jacy's expression changes. The fear is gone, replaced by

something else. His genius brain, thinking madly, has come up with a plan.

"You're right," he says. "I'm not much of a superhero. But Ali—"

Another smash to the face. Rage deepens Ryan's voice. "Her name is Ali*cia!*"

Blood drips from Jacy's mouth. His eyes search for mine. I can't tell whether he sees me or not. Doesn't matter.

I know exactly what he wants me to do.

There's only one chance to get it right. With as unobtrusive a movement as possible, I shift so that I'm directly in front of Ryan. With Jacy to my left, my feet slide into fifth position. Just like Quentin preaches, I shift my entire weight onto the back leg…waiting…waiting…

"I'm sorry, Mr. Ryan," Jacy tells him. "What I meant to say is, Alicia is Batman's Queen!"

No hesitation. The instant he says the last word, Jacy ducks out of the way. My forward leg comes up at the same time. High, fast, straight. A perfect grande battement. Toes pointed, aiming directly for the spot underneath Ryan's chin.

Shoe crunches bone. Ryan's head snaps up and back. His knees buckle, and he collapses onto the tar-paper roof.

The rest of the night is a blur. Sirens, police, somebody cuts the tape around my wrists but I don't remember who.

The one thing I'm certain about, though, is Jacy's excitement. As soon as Ryan went down, I pulled the cable from Jacy, grabbed his arm, and we hustled into the stairwell. He couldn't stop talking.

"Once I got onto the roof and locked onto you, Ali, I was *there.* I could tell when he pulled you away, where he stopped, when he got close again. I couldn't see, but I knew. It wasn't only sounds, either. I sensed it. How scared you were, how crazy he is..."

My knees are like Jell-O. Jacy feels that, too. He puts his arm around me and leads me to the elevator.

Confidently, like he knows just how many steps it will take.

chapter forty-six

I take my last final exam on a beautiful summer-solstice afternoon. Algebra II. Jacy made me study forever, so I'm confident I passed.

It's also the day we find out Ryan will, indeed, be sentenced to prison. Charlie's video was more than enough proof for the police to search the apartment. The cops found plenty of footage of me, and my room, on both the desktop computer and the laptop. He even shot the calendar where I wrote *BALTIMORE* across the weekend, as well as some of my dolls.

After examining the angles on Ryan's monitor, the police found the second camera in the smoke detector. They ripped it out, and took down the street cam, too.

The district attorney told us that Mr. Ryan's windpipe will never be the same. Nobody, including Mom, seems at all upset by that news.

The oddest thing of all, however, is what happened to my friends after Ryan was arrested. It's like everyone felt this need to try something new.

Clarissa not only helped make costumes for the school's

production of *The Tempest*—she got a tiny part as a member of the shipwrecked crew.

Sonya came out of the intellectual closet in Ms. Hebenstreit's English class. In answer to a question about the damaged characters in *Ethan Frome,* she gave a mini-lecture that startled everyone. The way Clarissa tells it, Josh got into it with her and Sonya brought him to his metaphorical knees. Guess she's not crushing on him anymore.

Luke dropped out. Laura Hernandez told Sonya he's planning to take the high school equivalency test and head out to California. Alone.

Charlie decided it would be smart to stop volunteering in the computer lab. Second semester, he took Creative Writing to fill the time. Instead of shooting stuff for Zube, he's writing a screenplay about gymnast thieves who break in to apartments.

"It'll be epic," he assures us.

Nobody doubts him.

Jacy wants to celebrate the last day of school with a picnic on the roof. "Just you and me, Ali. Nobody else."

It's the first time I've been there since *that night,* but it's turned into his favorite place. Carefully, he lays a blanket on the tar paper, places his cane on the edge so he can find it when it gets dark and sets down his laptop. I busy myself with the food.

"Música, por favor!" I say.

Jacy clicks his computer. I hand him a fresh mozzarella-and-tomato sandwich.

"Bread's from Fondue Junction. The olive kind you like so much."

"Cool." He eats half the sandwich before clearing his

throat. "I've got news. The *Voice* is giving me the summer internship. I pitched an idea about advances in gene therapy and they want me to research it. There's a chance it could work for a couple of different eye diseases." His dimples deepen as he grins. "Plus, I've decided to go back to WiHi next year. I want to graduate with everyone."

"Yes! Homecoming, prom—"

"Hey! I'm not agreeing to do everything."

I take a delicate bite of sandwich. "Whatever."

He eyes me. "You're not going to argue?"

"You'll do it all. You'll see."

I snuggle into him. I've become quite a good kisser over the past six months. Then again, I've taken lessons from the best.

We listen to music, finish our sandwiches and watch the sun deepen its glow—until a song comes on that I haven't heard in months. The Clash. A punch in the gut. I fumble for the laptop's stop button.

"If I'm going to school in the fall," Jacy says softly, "don't you think you ought to go back to the studio?"

"I told you. I'm never dancing again."

"Why? Ryan can't bother you anymore."

I turn away. The topic is not up for discussion.

"If you don't go back, he's won," Jacy says. "You know that, right?"

"I don't care."

Jacy stops me from packing up the food. "Ali? Can I ask for one favor?"

"What?"

"I never got to see the whole solo."

"Jace—"

"Please." He gives me the puppy-dog pout I've never been able to resist. "I won't ask again. Promise."

"You want me to show you now? Right here? I haven't stretched in ages."

"So stretch."

The water tower becomes a barre. As I warm up, I try to keep my heart from racing. The events of *that night* are in sharp focus. *There* is where Ryan tossed the mints, *that* is where I was afraid he'd push Jacy off the roof—and *this* is where he threw me to the ground.

I freeze midplié. I can't do it. When I turn to tell Jacy, he's making another sandwich. His head is bent low so he can see.

Sometimes one person's courage is greater than another's fear.

If I'm going to do the solo right, I need the chain belt. By the time I get it from my room, however, it'll be too dark. Right now, the sky makes a perfect backdrop—a tapestry of red, orange, purple.

I look for something to use as a substitute. The only thing close is a piece of cable. I hesitate—that's what Ryan tied Jacy up with—but there's nothing else. I make Jacy turn around, wrap it around my waist and mark the piece. Funny the way I remember every step.

When I'm ready, he taps the computer's keypad and the song fills the air.

I hit the beginning poses with precision, do my two grande battements and slip into the arabesque to hold for the tempo change. When it comes, the music propels me into the Martha Graham contraction—and the part I never performed.

I dance with abandon. For Jacy. And maybe, just maybe, for myself.

The song draws to a close. The way it was originally choreographed, I turned my back to the audience before the final chord, wrapped the chain around my face and then revolved to face front.

Prisoner, slave, caged animal.

But this time, as I make the turn, what has been hidden for so long becomes clear. Eva is right. Quentin's dances have nothing to do with pretty steps. He's saying something with them, far deeper than I realized. Despite despair and frustration, grief and disease, fear and longing, the heart keeps a steady beat.

That's when I understand why I dance. For some people, it's the only way to make sense of the past, to get to the meaning behind the present. To find your true self.

I slip the cable from my waist. Instead of wrapping it around my face, I hold it up and spin forward. The wire spans the multicolored sky. Arch. Rainbow. Bridge. Whatever the viewer sees is what I want them to see. What I allow them to see.

The audience of one explodes into applause. With a graceful bow, I savor the knowledge that I've just given the finest performance of my life.

Deep down, I know it won't be my last.

★ ★ ★ ★ ★

Acknowledgments

I owe a debt of gratitude to many people.

On the East Coast: The Rosenfeld-McCarthy family (Ruthie, Edmund, Maya), dancer Sarah Safford, The Maeby/Cashin families for my own private Yaddo, my indefatigable agent, Alison Picard, my fab, and fun, editor Adam Wilson, Natashya Wilson and the rest of the Harlequin Teen crew.

On the West Coast: Betty Gottsdanker, Nora Rohman, the California State Summer School for the Arts, Danny Rosenberg and Dr. Eric Takeshita (technical advice), Claire Carmichael at UCLA Extension, Donna May, YA authors Sally Nemeth, C. Leigh Purtill, Mark London Williams and Eric Talkin. As always, fellow writers Jack and Liana Maeby were awesome beyond belief, along with Dylan Maeby (the rock of our family).

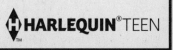

Facebook.com/HarlequinTEEN

Be first to find out about new releases,
exciting sweepstakes and special events
from Harlequin TEEN.

Get access to exclusive content,
excerpts and videos.

Connect with your favorite
Harlequin TEEN authors and fellow fans.

All in one place.

Facebook is a registered trademark of Facebook, Inc.

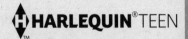